PEPPER

INSPIRED ROMANCE

SINMISOLA OGÚNYINKA

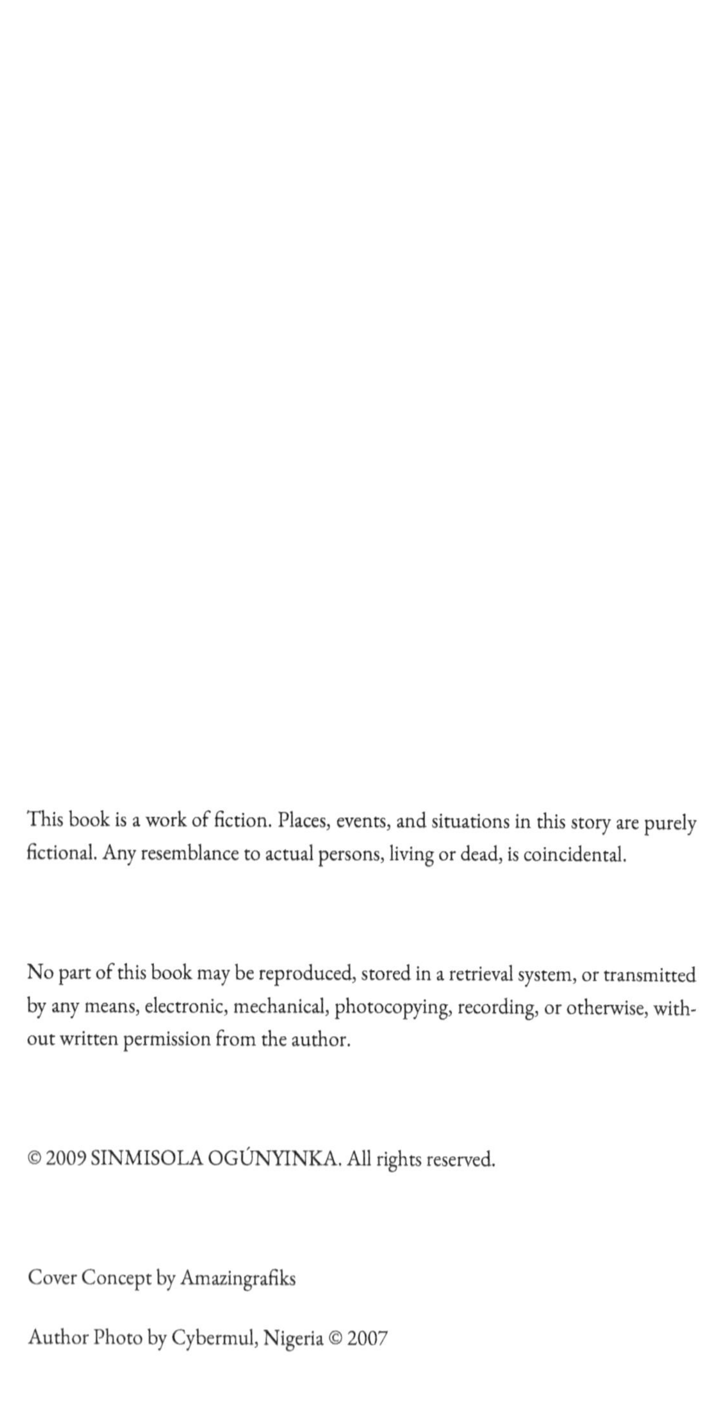

This book is a work of fiction. Places, events, and situations in this story are purely fictional. Any resemblance to actual persons, living or dead, is coincidental.

No part of this book may be reproduced, stored in a retrieval system, or transmitted by any means, electronic, mechanical, photocopying, recording, or otherwise, without written permission from the author.

Cover Concept by Amazingrafiks

Author Photo by Cybermul, Nigeria © 2007

Dedicated to my Salts and Peppers

Ife and Iyin

Aanu and Oore

1

— · —

Pam zipped up her dress in front of the mirror she and Elle had shared for half their lives. "If it starts to rain, I'll go crazy."

"I don't know why you swear all the time, Pam," Elle mumbled trying not to disturb the make-up artist working on her face.

"It's for you, sister," Pam said tartly. "I couldn't care less if the heavens decided to do over time today. It's your wedding, not mine."

"Yeah right," Elle talked properly, and the artist muttered a complaint.

"If you talk again, I'll have to wash your face and start all over," the young man said. Elle felt uncomfortable having the guy all over her face and hated the rebuke.

"Tell my sister to shut up, not me," she said edgily.

Pam turned from looking in the mirror, and at the young man. "Why should you talk to Elle like that? Are you mad?" she said. "If you cannot do your job then get out!"

"Good God, Pam," Elle said softly, hiding a smile.

From the day they both got expelled from their mother's body, five minutes apart, Pam had fought Elle's battles. In fact, their mother often told them Elle came out first without crying, and then Pam came with her hand first, clenched; screaming like hell was loose. Her crying jolted the quiet Elle and despite the efforts to make Elle cry at the first, she did not until her sister was out, and wailing.

"I was just trying to..."

"Just apologise or leave," Pam spat.

"I'm sorry. Please try and stay still," the sullen guy said.

Elle smiled. "It's okay."

Their mother, a rotund woman in her early fifties walked in, all decked up and ready for the occasion. She opened and twisted her heavy george wrapper back into place as she swept the room with one quick glance.

"You girls are still not ready?"

Elle spoke up. "In a minute, Mummy."

"Don't wait for us," Pam said.

So like them, so predictable in their words and actions. Their mother smiled. "Today is a great day, Emmanuelle. God has honoured you," she said. "Oh, if only your father were to be here!" she sighed and dabbed the sudden watery eyes.

Pam pulled her into her arms in a genuine show of affection. "Dad is here, smiling at us." She cleared her throat and resumed her strong presence. "Now Elle let this man finish your face so you get to church before the rain starts."

"Go ahead, Mummy. We're right behind you," Elle said.

Her make-up artist stepped back to look at her. "Perfect." He quickly packed his bag.

"Thank you," Elle said.

"Briefly look at your face before you wear your gown now" Pam said, standing beside her and admiring her. "You look gorgeous. Akim will not be able to take his eyes off you today."

"And always, I hope," Elle whispered.

Pam gave her air a kiss. "Of course, baby."

Their mother stood at the entrance of the room and smiled in joy and sadness. Their father had been killed in an auto accident a few months earlier, causing pain and anguish in the family.

Joe Ukpabi had been a great father and husband. God had in His infinite mercy blessed him with just this set of twins and he had taken good care of them. He had been on his way back from work on that terrible July day, and while trying to avoid a child, who suddenly ran across the road, driven into a ditch. He had died of shock according to the medical report.

It was truly a disaster for the family. Joe had always talked of giving his daughters out in marriage. It had been his dream throughout all his sixty-one years alive. At his burial, the reverend Theophilus Uka had described him as a saint, and challenged those he left behind to emulate his righteous living.

"He has joined the great cloud of witnesses in heaven, and he is urging us on..."

A small noise wafted through the corridor of the house to the bride's room, jolting Glory Ukpabi out of her reverie. Joe's junior brother, Eddie, who would give the bride away, was ready and calling on her to hurry the girls.

"You know Rev. Uka hates late coming!" Eddie said.

"They are ready!"

Elle slipped into her wedding dress. The beautiful dress was made from a patchwork of ivory satin and lace. It had an illusion halter neckline with the bare back, and shoulders covered with lace patched shawl. The princess cut carved the beautiful figure down to a full bodice, and an elaborate train.

Elle and Pam had chosen the style by combining three elegant styles they found in a bridal website. Elle's veil was a short ensemble that barely covered her face when flung over. It added a dash of whimsy to the gown.

Their first cousin, who was also a renowned fashion designer, had burnt her midnight candle perfecting the gown. Elle wore white gloves that reached up to her upper arm effectively covering some of the otherwise exposed flesh. She slid into her high-heeled white sandals and turned to her sister. Pam fitted a tiara on her sister's head and stepped back to assess it. It was lovely.

Pam took a deep breath. "Are you ready for this?" She felt as nervous as her sister.

"Yes sis. Oh yes." Elle breathed in and hugged her sister, and turned to hug their mother who still stood admiring her only two children. "Let's go!" She hurried toward the door only to turn and see her sister and mother standing back and staring at her.

"I'll cry and spoil this make-up just now," she said, and they moved simultaneously toward her exclaiming, and erupting in laughter.

The video man engaged to cover the occasion came to them and started moving backward slowly, covering the procession. When they all got to the sitting room, photographs were taken.

"The next time you walk into this house, you'll be married," Pam told her and giggled excitedly. "Where are the ladies of honour and little bride?"

"Here," someone called out as two ladies in identical pink dresses walked in with a little girl, wearing the miniature version of Elle's dress. She carried a bouquet identical to one earlier thrust into the bride's hands.

"Ok, let's take the pictures and go," Eddie growled. His wife pinched him by the side and asked him to calm down; after all, they still had twenty minutes left before the service started.

For several minutes they grouped and re-grouped. The photographer insisted on getting everyone taken till Eddie sulkily went to sit in the car, and wait them out.

When Elle finally joined him, it was obvious she would be late to church on her wedding day. She squeezed her uncle's hand and settled into the car, with Pam and the little bride seated in front.

"Uncle, I'm sorry," she murmured soberly. Her remorse moved him.

He smiled at her. "You're the most beautiful bride I have ever seen."

2

—·—

How someone could wear such a dress, he wondered.

The lilac cocktail-length a-line dress clung to her slim but endowed figure. The flung champagne shawl across her bare back and shoulders exposed by the halter-neckline, and low cleavage dress only drew more attention to her lovely smooth skin than otherwise, as the piece of detail continually shifted away from its position.

Lilac and champagne coloured roses were woven into an otherwise disarray hair, allowing the roughly set waves freedom they probably craved. She wore very high lilac sandals that exposed how long and beautiful her legs were. This was a very unusual maid of honour. Her pretty face was neatly but lightly made up with earth colours.

He drew in a deep breath and looked back in the wedding program, from the elevated area the officiating ministers sat, facing the congregation; wondering which verse they were now at. The bride was more decently dressed than her maid of honour.

Why would these ladies not dress properly, especially on days like this, when there were so many visitors in the church? Recently, he started to implement the wedding gown rule in his parish. Now he perfectly understood why pastors insist on seeing the wedding dresses and those of the bridal train before the wedding day.

He gazed unseeing at the program, just as the bride reached the altar, singing the last line of the processional hymn. He looked up and his eyes did a misfit with the maid of honour's. It was a passing glance but he couldn't take his eyes off her face.

She had the most remarkable features he'd ever seen. Her eyes were large, oval-shaped, and with dark brown lining, more highlighted. She had a typical African nose, though smaller than usual and full lips, accentuated by the lining of her lips and deep brown lipstick. The lip gloss she applied made her mouth look wet. Temptingly. Her cheeks were smooth like porcelain, her eye brows were perfectly shaped; her cheekbone perfectly chiselled, and high.

She bent slightly to arrange the elaborate train so the bride could sit easy, oblivious of his stupefaction, and he just gazed at her. The dress is too tight, he thought wearily.

Rev. Theo Uka, a once-handsome man in his late fifties took the call to worship, and declaration of purpose. A younger priest took an opening prayer, and the reverend came back to do the joining of the couple. After all the ceremonies and charges, the officiating ministers were asked to pray for the couple.

Obasse stood up from his seat and along with eight other clergies, surrounded the couple and prayed for them. Afterward, the choir came up and rendered an amazing piece. Obasse then climbed the pulpit after the choir rounded up their number, insisting within himself it was perfectly normal to look at the couple, and whoever was with them.

Pamelle. He'd checked the names on the bridal train for hers. She was the bride's twin and they were almost identical. Emmanuelle was slightly more slender than her twin but Pamelle's waist was so small, accentuated by the reveal of her dress.

He'd also noticed the best man could not keep his eyes off her. And several times, he sited them chatting mutedly. During the declaration, they'd both been looking at her. And whilst they prayed for the couple, he'd made conversation with her. And now as he climbed the pulpit, he noticed they were talking again.

Why would they be so undisciplined in the church? From the way the best man looked at and talked to her, he knew they were not previously acquainted. Akim had told him his best man was a friend from childhood who'd made a living in Lokoja. He doubted if any of Akim's friends had ever met his best man before, including his bride or her family members.

"Shall we pray," he said briefly into the microphone left on the pulpit. The prayer was brief and he ensured his eyes were closed through it.

"When I was growing up as a young believer, I found one song very intriguing because it was usually sung on wedding days like this," he started. "And because I haven't yet heard it sung today, I think I want to raise it." He looked toward the choir stand. "Can I get a help from the choir?"

A few of the choir members stood up to stand at the back-up microphone stands. "Please celebrate this choir for me. The piece was wonderful," Obasse said and there was a loud applause. "The song says, 'I'm married to Jesus Satan leave me alone. Do we know it, choir?" There were shy nods from the back-up singers. "Right. I thought you would," he teased.

"But before we take it, what intrigues me the most is that, I never thought the composer wanted it to be a wedding day song, as such, but that's what we turned it into. And so you hear things like, I'm married to Akim, brothers leave me alone."

There was a roar of laughter. "And then they go; I'm married to Ella, sisters leave me alone." he laughed. "My husband is coming to take me away. To everlasting home! Can we take it together?"

The choir took it up and the congregation sang along. He looked at Pamelle. And she looked back at him.

"Halleluyah!" he shouted when the song ended. "Weddings are very special for me because I met Jesus at my sister's wedding. And because Jesus did his first miracle at a wedding, I believe Jesus loves to attend weddings, especially ones he's invited to.

"And he was invited to this wedding. I know it. The groom, Akim Duke is a friend and a parishioner who has proven to me over the years I've known him to love God. When he brought his bride to me, I noticed she has a calm and gentle spirit. It made me glad they are both Jesus lovers." He paused. "My simple message today is on the wedding invitation."

"Who did you or will you invite to your wedding? And subsequently, who have you invited to your marriage? The family at the wedding in Cana invited Jesus and ultimately, he saved the day for them. When the wine finished, he gave instructions; and when the instructions were followed, there was new wine poured, sweeter than the initial one. I have said quite a few significant things this day, and I want to elaborate on them one by one.

"Jesus was invited. From the beginning of the ceremony, Jesus was there. He wasn't just called hurriedly in at the last minute when it is too late. For many of us, we do still have a chance to invite Jesus in. As long as there is life, there is hope. And he said, come unto me and I will give you rest.

"The Bible says that it is appointed for a man to die once, and then the judgement. As long as you are alive, you can invite Jesus and he will honour your invitation. He said if you call upon me, I will answer you and deliver you from your troubles. This is the day of your salvation, tomorrow may be too late.

"The wine finished. Everything has an end, and when Jesus is not there, the end is really the end. Wine symbolises celebration, joy, peace, success, achievement and abundance. All these are essential for a good and happy married life. But then, inevitably, it finishes.

For some, the success brings distraction. The man stays more at work than at home; the woman cares more for the children than for her marriage. Wine finishes in every marriage. Sometimes, it is sudden death of a child or a close relative that dries up the wine. There are several reasons why the wine finishes and we must expect and prepare for it.

"The Bible tells us in the book of John 16 verse 33, that indeed in this world, we will face tribulations, but we should be of good cheer because he has overcome the world. That tells me that inevitably, the wine will finish.

"He gave instruction. Jesus gives instructions at every turn in life. He still speaks. Do you recognise his voice? He says that my sheep hear my voice and answer me.

"Many believers today have swapped the voice of their pastor for the voice of God so that when the pastor starts to make mistakes, they start to miss their way. Jesus still speaks. Everyday, I hear him speak to me. You need to relate with God for a blissful marriage. When he gives his instructions follow it. Don't murmur and grumble.

"Sometimes, his instructions are difficult and may look foolish. At the marriage in Cana, he asked them to pour water into the pots. He turned the chemistry to a mystery. But only after they obeyed him. Obedience is paramount to have a successful marriage.

"Brother Akim, if God tells you to buy that expensive jewelry for your wife, do it. Sister Ella, if he asks you to kneel and beg your husband, do it. He knows best and he will turn the chemistry in your marriage to a mystery." There's a loud chorus of 'Amen' from the congregation.

"There is new wine. I have heard many married people complain that it is impossible for their marriages to get sweet again. I hear women say their husbands are the devil reincarnate. I've heard men call their wives prostitute, witch and all manner of offensive words. Like water, words can not be retrieved when poured out. Even if you mop it up, a little still gets lost. But when Jesus is around to turn the chemistry to a mystery, all impossibilities become possible.

"Never limit the power of God in your home and in your marriage. He is able and more than able to restore the marriage to an even better, higher, and sweeter level than the first few weeks." He mopped sweat off his face. "Let me end my admonition with this story.

"A man invited Jesus to come and live in his house. He had his guest room prepared extensively and asked Jesus to stay there. At night, thieves came to the house and left the downstairs guest room, and went upstairs to raid.

"When they left, the man cried to Jesus, why? Why did you allow thieves to come up and steal from me, after I gave you the most beautiful room in the house? Jesus replied him and said, 'I guarded the room you gave me. I wasn't asked to leave the room.' The man said, 'Ok. I do understand that. Please stay in the whole of the ground floor so you'll see if they are coming or not and you can block them.'

"That same night, the thieves returned, and seeing Jesus in the parlour downstairs, they climbed through the backside of the house upstairs and raided the house again.

"When they left, the man was distraught but he did not ask Jesus any questions. He said, 'Master, take the whole house and put me where you like. As long as you are in charge, I am safe.' And so when the thieves came that night for another operation, they could not gain access to the house. Jesus was in charge everywhere!" A loud halleluyah interrupted the message.

"Behold he stands at the door and knocks. He wants to come into your life and marriage. He wants to turn all the waters in your life into wine. He wants to make a change for you. Where will you put him? When will you heed his call?

"Every marriage has a great potential with Jesus. Without him, it has failed already. I want us to rise up on our feet as I make two calls. Be sincere and answer Jesus today.

"Somebody's knocking at your door. Somebody's knocking at your door. Oh oh sinner, why don't you answer. Somebody's knocking at your door," he sang softly. His baritone voice was strong and sweet but he stopped after singing only once.

"You want to give your life to Jesus, please come out. God loves you and he wants you. God bless you my sisters, God bless you my brothers. Do you want to invite Jesus into your home and your marriage, please come forward?

"He's the only one able to solve all our problems; able to turn the bitterness and wateriness and sourness of our marriages to sweet wine. God bless you as you surrender all to him. I wish to invite our father and reverend to pray for us. Please may the rest of the congregation pray for these ones who have come out." He turned and handed over the microphone to Rev. Uka with a slight bow. He took his seat, and noticed that the altar was crowded with people. He thanked God for the harvest and mopped sweat off his face.

Pamelle stole a glance at him then, but he didn't notice.

3

T he rain finally emptied its bowels later in the evening. The Duke family had organized an elaborate after wedding party at the patriarch's residence where Akim and Elle were the special guests. Pam followed as part of her duty to her sister. The best man, Osita, was also invited.

Whilst the bride and groom were being celebrated, Osita tried to make an impression on Pam. He and Akim came a long way and had been friends since their high school days. Then they had promised that they would be best man for one another. Osita had studied medicine while Akim went the opposite way to study a family profession, Accounting.

The years after university had finally separated them geographically, but the two kept in touch with one another. Osita practiced medicine in Lokoja, and had been only too glad to shelve his busy schedule to fulfil his part of the agreement.

"I hope your wife won't be in labour the day I want to get married," he had teased Akim over the phone.

"That shouldn't be a problem," Akim said. "We'll all come all the same, and have the baby at your wedding!"

But seeing Pam, he was more grateful for coming. He had had a series of failed relationships due to his 'play boy' attitude but he now wanted to settle down. And with who else but his maid of honour.

He knew several couples who'd met like this. In fact, many people look out for the best man and maid of honour after the wedding. So, as Pam escorted Elle during the party, Osita, clung to Akim. And Pam.

He liked her. She was savvy, outgoing, and they had a lot in common. After exchanging addresses and phone numbers, he continued to bond with her. He was sure she liked him too.

When the first drops of the rain began, everyone went indoors to continue the party, and soon the two large sitting rooms in the house were filled with people. Elle and Akim moved around the guests, chatting and socializing. They were both very tired after the long day and wanted to escape quickly. They found the opening when Akim's mother beckoned on them to sit and eat.

"We'll eat in the room," Akim suggested quickly.

"Okay. What will you take? There's everything, from variety of rice to pounded yam and fufu," she said, beckoning on one of the young waitresses.

"I'll take coconut rice and fish with coke," Elle said.

"I'll take some fried rice and plenty of assorted meat," Akim said. "And any kind of juice. Good God, it's my first meal to-day!"

"I'll have your order brought to your room," his mother said and made to leave.

Elle sat up abruptly. "Mummy please, I don't know where Pam is but please could you help us call her too?"

"I saw her cornered somewhere with Osita…" Akim said and chuckled. "Please find them so they can also join us to eat."

Akim's mother moved to the door and turned the handle. "Ok. No problem."

Akim wrinkled his nose. "It can't work between them."

Elle raised her newly-shaped eyebrows. "Why do you say that? He seems smitten by her."

"They're too much alike. Their lives will be boring."

"If they don't kill themselves first."

She smiled and he tickled her.

He opened his neatly arranged room for her and they both entered. The air conditioner had been left on for them, and the room was chilling.

When they got home from the reception ceremony, they had both hurriedly changed from their wedding outfits to a baby green lace combination. Elle wore hers in the native richly beaded oyonyon while Akim wore his as the chieftaincy shirt, and tied the traditional wrapper. They had danced briefly before retiring to their room to eat.

While away at the party, Akim's mother had arranged for their wedding dress and suit to be tidied away and the room cleaned again. The emperor-size bed was neatly made with lovely plain and patterned indigo bed sheet.

Elle dropped on the bed spread-eagled, tired and Akim dropped right on top of her, stilling her giggle with hot kisses.

There was a knock on the door and before they could answer, the door opened. Elle made to push her husband off but he held her down. Pam entered the room with Osita on her tow and stopped short.

"Are we interrupting something?" she asked stoically.

"Not yet. We're still dressed," Akim said flagrantly and Elle shoved him off. He reluctantly moved away and fell on his back on the bed. "I'm not hungry anymore!" he groaned. "At least not for food." He squeezed his eyes shut and Pam and Osita walked fully into the room anyway.

"Well, you sent for us and that's why I'm not going back out there."

"Your father's house is across town, Pep. I'm in mine," Akim said and sat up in one fluid movement. He pulled Elle into his arms and kissed her soundly.

"You can't chase us out of here, bro." Pam took a seat at the reading table. "I'm tired and famished."

Another knock on the door, and Elle called to come in. Two waitresses brought the food and drinks into the room and set them on a side table.

"Please serve," Elle said and shifted a little away from Akim. Osita took another seat close to Pam and the company waited quietly, placing their orders for food. When the servers had left, they gobbled their food quietly for a while.

"This is what I love most about weddings," Osita started. "The wedding night."

"Hmm," Akim grumbled. "Without interruption, you mean."

"You sent for us. You knew you wanted to be alone, why did you send for us?" Pam snickered.

"Elle wanted you not me."

"Goodness, Akim. We both wanted them!"

"No way. I wanted my wife, she wanted her sister." He took a huge swallow of juice, and belched.

Elle started to say something but shook her head. "God, husband. What a husband."

"Any regrets yet?" Osita teased.

"A trailer load. I should follow Pam back to her father's house."

Akim raised his hand in mock excitement. "I'll go with you."

Pam sat forward. "Are you still leaving after church tomorrow morning?"

Elle shrugged. "I have no choice as you can see. The husband won't wait a moment longer."

Pam shrugged. "I'm going to miss you badly. But you'll be back in a week anyway."

"I wish I could stick around and keep you company for the week but I have to go back also," Osita said.

Akim arched his eyebrows. "Tomorrow?"

"I'm looking at Monday. Pam and I thought we should spend a little time together tomorrow."

"That's wonderful!" Elle winked at Pam, who rolled her eyes. "We'll take the afternoon flight out to Lagos and then go to Ghana."

"That's wonderful. I hope the thanksgiving service will be short enough?" Osita asked.

"It lasts the normal time. Our flight is for 3pm so there's time." Akim jumped to his feet. "That reminds me, I haven't gotten the tickets yet!"

"We can call my cousin Obia. She works at the airport," Elle said.

"I'll call." Pam offered and dialled on her handset. She stood up and walked to the corner of the room to make the call, only to return after a few seconds. "She said it's no problem. She'll make sure we have two seats."

"Together!" Akim said.

"Well, you can't do much in the plane can you?" Pam retorted.

"I can't blame you twin sister," Akim mumbled. "You're not yet married!"

Osita stood up. "Well, I guess we should leave you two then. Since my friend is getting saucy. It can be for only one reason."

"It's late and I don't think it's good to drive at this time," Elle said.

Akim yawned. "With the house so full, they'll probably have to sprawl on the couch, if they find it."

"We'll drive. It's only after midnight," Osita said. "I'll drop her at the house before going to my hotel."

Elle looked at the best man. "Where are you staying?"

"Uncle's guest house at the Marina Resort," Akim said. "And he has my car to use."

"No, it's too late for that distance..."

"It's not. Let's go." Pam pulled Osita up, and they both headed out.

"Well, let's see them off, husband." Elle pulled Akim off the bed as well, and they all headed out. They took a back door to avoid the thronging guests, out of the house to where Osita had parked his car in the morning. The two sisters stood apart as the friends talked. They would not see much of each other the following day.

"Remember to bring that my old cardigan from the house, please," Elle said softly.

"I will. I'll just go and pack it now. Is there any other thing you need?"

"I don't think so. I'm packing this night before we sleep so I'll let you know if there's anything."

"Are you guys leaving for the airport from here or Akim's house?"

"I don't know yet. I'll tell you in church tomorrow."

Pam rubbed her nose. "I ... I won't come for the thanksgiving."

"Why?!"

"Just send a text and let me know."

"Why won't you come? Mom and the rest of the family are even understandable ..."

"That pastor. Akim's pastor!"

"Pastor Obasse? What about him? You don't like his preaching?"

Pam hissed. "He kept looking at me. Even during his sermon."

"Looking how? They were sitting where they could look at everybody. He kept looking at me and smiling too."

"He wasn't smiling when he looked at me."

"So?" Elle laughed incredulously. "I didn't notice anything. How many times did you catch him looking at you?"

"Uncountable."

"Which means you were looking at him too," Elle accused lightly.

"Of course, after I noticed he was looking at me, I stared right back, just to get his eyes off me."

Elle laughed out. "And did it work?"

"Sure. But then I will look away and he would just start staring right back!" Pam hissed again. "I hated it. It was like his eyes were crawling all over me…"

"Ladies?" Osita called.

Akim walked over and rudely interrupted them. "Baby, leave this spinster alone and let's go do what married people do."

"I bet you, Pam, he won't do anything o, despite all the harassment." She spanked her husband playfully.

"Send the text," Pam said.

Akim dragged Elle along.

"Oh no. Please come. Please!" Elle called back. And shouted, "Thank you!!!"

They entered the house.

4

—·—

She wore a burgundy skirt suit that threw him completely off balance. But he had promised himself he would never look at her again if by any chance they met. And he did not. She came into the church with her mother and went to hug her sister straight off. They caused a small distraction as they settled down. The good thing however was that they'd come on time just as the service was about to begin.

After that first glance, which thankfully he noticed from the safe confines of his office through the reflexive window, he took his eyes away from her. Since he now knew where she sat, he promised himself he would not look at that side of the church hall. But he stole a quick glance at her again. Goodness, what a lady!

Her hair was neatly untidy, brushed into soft waves. He noticed it was quite long, or could it be artificial hair? He doubted it. She leaned over to talk to the man beside her... the best man! What was he doing here? Well, what was he not? Pamelle smiled at something he said and leaned over him slightly as a show of fondness. Obasse swallowed and cleaned his face with a white handkerchief, leaning his head back on his seat.

The praise worship started and he began to speak in tongues softly. There was a lot on his mind right now. The letter posting him to another parish was lying on his table and he was working on a handover note due to be submitted the following day. Yet, he had a trailer load of reports to read through. He was resuming in the new parish the following Sunday and he had to have a good knowledge of the workings of the parish.

Today he would officially hand over his parish to his assistant who would now be the parish pastor. The emotional impact of that in itself was much for him. He had grown to love the workers and members of this church which he started in as an assistant pastor five years earlier. His new parish was bigger and there had been a strong debate on whether it was appropriate to send him, a bachelor, to pastor such a congregation. But then, he had an impeccable record.

Over the years, he had ensured he guarded his integrity jealously. Anything beyond the four walls of the scriptures became a no-go area for him. And this had preserved him.

Obasse packed his Bible and sermon notebook and stood up with a sigh. This was Sunday morning, his hour of call. Long ago he had swapped Sunday for Monday in his calendar and now worked the reverse.

On Sunday, he worked hard full day. On Monday, played football and slept half of the day. Though since his transfer, he had not been able to indulge in the luxury. His congregation of two hundred adults and about half that number of children was a growing one.

He had worked with his assistant as pastor-in-charge for three years after the former pastor relocated to another state because of his secular employment. The church had only grown stronger since then. He would have loved to stay on a little longer but the pastor in the new church decided to go into full-time itinerant village evangelism, which drew a huge respect from everyone.

Obasse Edim had not always been a pastor. Previously, he worked as a public relations officer for a private high school, a job which contradicted his calm and quiet personality. But when it came to the job, he attacked it headlong, viewing his challenges, talking mainly, as stepping stones.

He was a man of very few words, and this reflected even in his messages. However, he had the divine capability of passing across his message in clear and simple terms, a trait which endeared his congregation to him. Several of them walked up to him to express how much they would miss him, but then they also loved their assistant pastor, and that was the consolation.

The church auditorium, arranged in four distinctive rows was packed full when Obasse climbed the altar. He reminded himself quickly not to look, much as he was tempted to do so, in Pamelle's direction. He'd noticed how she returned his looks the previous day, with initially respectful ones, which he later noticed became curious and finally scornful. Who would like to be stared at the way he had. He just couldn't explain... well he could. She was an unusual person. Summary.

The thanksgiving service went smoothly without incident. Until the head of the couples' fellowship announced that the new couple would be hosted to a surprise dinner party at a leading Chinese restaurant later on. Akim reacted first, shaking his head, refuting.

After service, Elle followed him into Obasse's office to take the excuse.

"Pastor please... we're travelling today, after lunch," Akim said as he burst into Obasse's office, startling the pastor.

"Oh God, I didn't know," Obasse said apologetically. "I wasn't even aware of the dinner till this morning."

Akim shook his head. "Can it be postponed till next week? We'll be back next week Sunday."

"I am not sure... wait, let me call Brother Titus. Please sit down," he said softly and left the office.

Pamelle stood at the entrance of the door with Osita, chatting. She stiffened when Obasse came out and almost bumped into her.

"Sorry," he mumbled, disoriented for a second.

She stepped away from him without a word and he moved into the church to fetch Bro. Titus, the head of the couples' fellowship, followed closely by Akim and Elle. It was hard not to notice his nice height and handsome build. He was all masculine, if you'd ever seen one with at least four inches above her 5'7. His dark complexion was a bit unusual for their tribe but it was the clean, shiny type that depicted ebony, or black beauty. His skin was firm and quite hairy. He was slight in frame, but with great potential to add a few necessary kilos. He felt her eyes on him as he stood respectfully in front of Bro. Titus.

"No no no. It's not possible sir. Please. I am ready to pay the charges for cancelling the booking," Titus said in a demanding tone.

"The main problem is the ticket for the flight to Ghana," Elle said quietly.

"Exactly." Akim nodded. "We've not even bought the local ticket but the…"

"Give me your agent's number," Titus said. Reluctantly, Akim gave him. Titus moved out of the pastor's office and returned a few moments later. "Your flight has been rescheduled for tomorrow," he announced victoriously. "So we'll see you at the royal Chinese restaurant this evening at 6?"

"Yes sir. Thank you."

Obasse noticed Akim was not too excited about the change. "It's okay. They mean well," he murmured after Titus had left the office.

"We'll take our leave then." He looked round at his small party.

*

"What are we going to be doing there?" Pam's eyes widened. "It's a couple's night out for crying out loud."

"It will be a good time to relax. It's the reason why I'm staying till tomorrow," Osita said calmly.

"Well, I'm not going to sit and listen to married stuff in a couples' dinner!" Pam raised her voice. "Look, what if they start doing dancing competition or some silly things, what will we be doing?"

Osita shrugged. "Talking and getting to know ourselves better I guess."

Pam hissed. "Yeah right! Not in some couples' thing, I won't."

"Talk to her guys. I'm doing this for her," Osita said, trying to be jovial. Pam snickered.

"Well?"

"Well, she'll go with you. If she wants," Akim said.

They were headed for Akim's house and Pam positively lost her temper after Osita accepted the invite to come along for the couples' outing.

"That doesn't sound so encouraging," Osita groaned. "So where do we go this evening then?"

"I don't think I want to go anywhere." Pam sulked.

Her attitude irritated Osita and he couldn't hide it in the steely tone. "We can stay home then. Have a quiet dinner..."

"I don't feel much like entertaining." She looked at him. "I'm tired and I just want to be alone."

"Huh, just the mood I dreaded," Elle said.

"Please don't start, Elle. I hate the attention!" Pam snapped.

"I'll probably start out today," Osita mumbled. "I could spend the night at Obudu."

"Of course not, Osita. She'll come out of the foul mood," Akim said.

"What if she doesn't? My night would be wasted. I'll be lonely and regretting my decision. If I set out this afternoon, I'll be at the hospital tomorrow before noon. At least I've saved half a day." Osita shrugged.

"Goodness gracious, you've allowed her to upset you." Elle turned to look at them both.

"Certainly not. She has a point anyway. None of us have been to this gathering before. It could get really embarrassing if they start to cosy up on couples..."

"But the couples' leader would not have invited you guys if it was going to be an ex-rated kind of outing as you both seem to paint it," Elle said.

"After all, Pam was the one who wondered how far we can go in the plane for just one hour," Akim added, smiling.

"Maybe when she's had lunch she will feel better and relax," Osita said, laughter in his voice.

The mockery in his tone was thick enough to cut.

"You should be trying to get her to come," Elle chided softly.

"Can't seem to see a way around it," Osita said. "What do you say, Pam?"

Pam hissed. "Please do what you please."

"See." Osita shrugged. "Can't really bend a rod when it is joined can you?"

Pam remained mute till they dropped Osita off at his hotel. When they went back to pick him up for the dinner, he had left. Pam, coincidentally, had decided at the last minute to surprise him!

5

He didn't relax until they walked in about twenty minutes late, and then he went all tense again when she followed them in. This time she wore a jade dinner gown with the notorious v-neck showing a little cleavage. The dress clung to all the curves in her body in a casual yet sensuous way. He did not place the curfew on his eyes anymore, and had a fill of her. Especially because his seat was at a far corner, where he sat with Bro. Titus and his wife, unnoticed by anyone walking in.

The trio were led first to the high table, where there were only two seats for the special guests, and then she was taken back into the crowd as the usher looked for an empty seat for her. There was an empty seat on his table and his heart quickened in fear and excitement. What was wrong with him?

Bro. Titus stopped the usher halfway to his table and asked the usher to create another space in front so the guests' guest could see clearly the high table and dance floor. That was when Obasse realised he had been holding his breath. The program progressed from there without incident. After a sumptuous buffet dinner, a toast was proposed. And the new couple were asked to take the dance floor. Most of the other couples joined them.

*

Pam did find out she was enjoying herself after the initial search for a seat which she found highly embarrassing. Akim had called Osita and she had spoken with him, apologising for her bad mood earlier. He said no offence was meant. They agreed he would visit her soon and she hung up. The food at the restaurant was good. The couples were doing great by ignoring her completely. Apparently, she felt she was the only single person in the room. The program had turned out to be very inspiring as the couples played several games, some making her laugh, and others sending her on a thinking trip. When the dance floor opened, she poured herself another glass of wine, and proceeded to relax and watch in amusement. Then he walked up to her table and smiled.

"Do you mind?" he asked politely, and took the seat which had been empty across her all along.

She hadn't been given the opportunity to accept or reject his request.

She shrugged. And then mumbled, "Please."

"Thank you," he said.

She sipped her drink, ignoring him totally. In her mind she battled her feelings and the great urge to tell him off.

"You are enjoying the evening?"

"Yes, thank you," she said and sipped again. He looked at her sister dancing with her husband and looked back at her. She refused to meet his gaze though she knew perfectly well he was staring at her. Let him look all he wanted, she thought angrily.

After worshipping in his church, she had formed a second opinion about him. And it wasn't flattery. He was the snobbish type. She now knew why he had stared at her so much the previous day. He was judging her. Sisters in his church covered their hair from ear to ear, few wore ear-rings and all wore skirts. No trousers on the ladies, and nothing but two- and three-piece outfits on the men.

"You're a very beautiful woman," he murmured into the glass of juice he'd brought with him. She pretended she hadn't heard him. "And you shouldn't be cold to me. I'm a friend of your family."

"Please Pastor, I really don't want to have this conversation, or any at that." She finally looked at him. He stared back.

"Why? We don't even really know ourselves that well."

"My point exactly. We have nothing in common."

He arched well-shaped eyebrows. "You're not born again?"

"Oh," she laughed spontaneously. Was he going to proceed to preach to her?

"Thanks for laughing. You've answered my question." He smiled again. He had a lovely smile she realised suddenly. He actually had a handsome face too, with dark, shiny skin and an oblong, clean-shaven face, and penetrating eyes, though she'd involuntarily noticed this the day before.

"Do you live here in Calabar?"

"Yes."

"I'll like to invite you to worship in our church on Tuesday," he said.

"What's the occasion?"

"Mid-week service."

Pam shook her head. "No way. I attend my church and it's fine with me."

The smile on his face lingered. "Why no way. Are you committed in your church that badly?"

"I can't come to your church, I don't have a scarf."

"I'll buy one for you," he said indulgently, watching her with those deep eyes. "Your sister will be in Ghana, and you'll need some comfort what do you think?"

"I don't need any comfort thank you." He made to answer but she stood up abruptly and smiled engagingly to the couple approaching the table, Elle and Akim. He turned on his seat in time to see them approach.

"Elle wants to take fresh air outside. We thought to tell you so you won't be worried," Akim said, glancing at Obasse. "I see pastor is cheering you up."

"He's not!" Pam said. "I was just trying to excuse him."

Elle's mouth dropped open. "Pam!"

"Well, then. Let's leave you to accomplish the feat," Akim said stiffly and led Elle out mumbling on the way, "One day, I'll clip her tongue."

Pam sat with a pout and turned away from Obasse, her body rigid on the seat.

"Tuesday is my last mid-week at the parish. I want you to be there," he said softly.

She had thought he would pursue her rudeness and bad attitude. His soft reply turned her gaze back to him, his intent, no doubt. She pouted, refusing to indulge him.

"Why are you so nervy? Or angry, is it?"

"Because you kept looking at me yesterday in the church."

"You noticed." It was a declaration.

"I hate people looking at me."

"Noted." He paused. She said nothing. "Will you be in church on Tuesday?"

"People like me don't attend churches like yours," she said tartly.

"How do you know? You visited only once, on a Sunday too," he said teasingly. "Alright. I won't ask you again," he said when she squeezed her face. They both sat silently and watched the couple dance.

She noticed he struggled to avert his gaze, and openly assessed him. It felt good to be on the giving end, she thought snugly.

6

It hadn't been easy for him to walk to her table Sunday night. And it wasn't easy now as he allowed the mini-logo orange Anne Klein jacquard scarf to wrap softly round his fingers, thinking of what was on his mind when he had offered the scarf. He had just bought the scarf at Sharon's boutique at an unexpected price. He didn't know scarves were sold in thousands of naira, but then it was a designer scarf. And he had refused to pick any of the cheaper ones he found.

For her.

But the scarf was now no longer a piece of designer clothing. It was a fleece. Would she come to church later in the evening? Would she wear anything matching the orange colour? If she did, then she was in his net. And if she didn't, waoh!

Orange was an extreme colour he had chosen only because of his purpose. If it didn't match, it didn't match. He had been tempted to buy black or grey or navy. Those were safe colours. Instead he picked the one with bright orange and tangelo shades. He had narrowed her options to black, white and orange.

"If she wears a pink dress..." He smiled at himself, and pulled himself together.

He hadn't slept much in the night. He'd been thinking and praying. He hated boomerangs, and if this one did, it would be too bad. He'd noticed since Saturday she wasn't a very cordial person. Her sister had scolded her softly when they returned from 'taking fresh air', and met them in stony silence. It wasn't that he couldn't make conversation with her despite her untoward attitude. He just didn't want to. He also liked being quiet. In fact, he'd discovered more words could be spoken in silence. When the couple joined their awkward fellowship, he'd politely excused himself, in order not to make them uneasy.

"That's not fair of you, Pam," Elle had rebuked softly, "Pastor is a nice person," she had said in his defence as he stood to leave them.

"I mean no offence." She shrugged nonchalantly.

"I am not offended. I enjoyed our conversation." He'd smiled and looked pointedly at her before turning to their company. "Have a blessed trip to Ghana."

"Thank you, Pastor," Akim said. "We'll call you when we arrive."

"That'll be great. Excuse me," he said, and left without looking at her again.

When he finally got round to dressing up, he said a quick prayer in front of the mirror. And assessed his outfit closely. Being finicky about what he wore had made his wardrobe turn out almost boring. Most of his clothes were in the family of blues greys and blacks. He also wore a lot of white shirts.

Normally, he dressed well on his meeting days because his pulpit was his office. Before choosing his tie, he'd rummaged through his wardrobe, finally settling for a black and blue striped silk tie. It was one of the best in his limited collection. He wore a white cotton shirt with a navy two-piece suit, with black belt and shoes.

Obasse was in the middle of his message when she walked in one hour late. He realised he hadn't told her the time the service started. Well, she came, and that was the good news. Someone had been reading a passage to him and he used the opportunity to signal to his protocol officer. Thankfully the passage was long.

The protocol took the small fancy bag to where she sat and she nodded. Immediately she opened it and brought out the lovely orange scarf, her head coming up to look at him sharply. A smile played on her lips and she shook her head in wonder, and he shyly smiled back, quickly picking his teaching up from where he'd left it off.

"So then faith is... and this is what I want to emphasize on. Your faith is a very present thing. It is. Faith is. Faith is not in your future, it is not in your past. It lives with you everyday. Faith is the substance of things hoped for; the evidence of things not seen." He stole a glance her way; she had tied the scarf round her neck. What a lady! Her head was bare, why didn't she tie the scarf on her head?

"Now let me explain this definition." He flipped through his Bible. "You hope to get admission after writing your examination, what gives you the admission is your faith. If you believe it, it is yours. You apply for a job and you *faith* that you have it.

It is substantial. Your faith makes you speak the things you have not seen as though you have. This is why it *is* the evidence of things not seen. Then you have the confidence to say, hey I got the job!" He laughed. "When in actual fact, you only just sat for the interview." Someone in the congregation raised their hand.

"You have a question?" He gesticulated toward a young man. "Let's have it."

"Sir, what if you end up not getting the job? Does it mean you were lying or what?"

"That's a very nice question. Now I have seen many Christians call things that are not as though they were. In fact, sometimes it becomes a joke. I am strong, we proclaim, and yet you are withering! I am rich, yet you trek home because you can't pay for a taxi ride. Now listen carefully to this," he said. "Your words mean nothing if they are not backed by faith. Many of us finish speaking the so-called faith talks and go ahead and contradict ourselves right after.

"Abraham was not thinking about any other thing when he gave Isaac up for sacrifice. We say we believe God will do it for us, yet we are thinking of one uncle or aunty. You shout I've got the job, thank Jesus, but you call your big brother who's in a position of influence right after. It is not a sin to call people to help you but don't lay it on faith. Having plans b, c and d is not wrong but don't feel like a mighty man of faith when you know you manipulated the outcome."

He looked around, and then focused his gaze on the young man. "Now to your question, the evidence of your faith is 'and it came to pass'. If you say you have faith, let us see it. You believe God for a child, let's see you get pregnant. Sometimes however, we may think it is faith. We sincerely call those things forth out of faith and really do believe God but God is sovereign and at times he delays the answer. Sometimes he refuses to answer and at times he answers in the negative to serve his purpose in your life. That's why the Bible says if you abide in Him and his word abides in you, then you will ask for what you want and it will be done to you."

Then she raised her hand and he swallowed hard.

"Yes please."

"Pastor, is it right to make your own plans. Play safe, take up only the things you can handle, live the way you can afford and leave the complications that go with having faith, out of your life?" Pam asked. She looked lovely in a short-sleeved orange, black and white block dress. The scarf matched as though the outfit was taken off a mannequin in a designer boutique.

"Wonderful question." He laughed. "I wish life was that simple but it isn't. It is not the question of right or wrong but rather if it is possible or not. John chapter number 16 and verse 33 says in this world, you will face tribulation. It is not a matter of choice. Through the tribulation, you need God and you need faith. Everything we get from God is a gift but sometimes we need to ask, we need to wait and we need to trust him.

"And in that, you have very little choice. You may make your own plans to go to your office in the morning and then it starts to rain heavily, you have to stay in or get an umbrella. You couldn't have stuck by your own plans then. So you need to plan with God and with faith. You can not live your life your own way. It is not possible. You need God, and the Bible says without faith, it is impossible to please God." He looked at her and nodded. "I believe that answers your question. Let us rise up on our feet. I want to invite us to our weekly Tuesday meetings. It is our teaching service and we look into the word of God deeply, exposing the truth. It is a believer's meeting and we interact and ask questions. It is a good opportunity to learn more for your everyday Christian living. I invite Pastor Tim to close the meeting," he said and left the pulpit.

Pastor Tim, the assistant pastor who would be taking over from him climbed the pulpit and began to sing, which led into the closing prayer. The members flocked round Obasse to wish him well since most of them would not be seeing him in their parish again. Pam waited in line till he finished with all the greetings and stepped forward.

"I just wanted to thank you for the scarf," she said briefly.

"I want to see you," he replied.

"Hope it is brief because my house is far from here and I didn't tell my Mummy I'll stay long," she said quickly. In fairness to her, she'd waited long enough just to thank him.

"I'll make sure you get home on time." He checked his watch. Blast! It was almost eight already. He wondered what was late and what was not for her. The town was safe though and commercial transporters worked till as late as ten. He didn't have a car but if need be, he would call any of his friends to come and take her home. It had to be tonight, he resolved.

"Please let's go into my office."

He walked away from the main auditorium into his office and she followed like a sheep to the slaughter.

"Please sit down." She did. He stood in front of her as though to deliver a lecture. She looked bored and uninterested in what he had to say until he did.

"I want you to be my wife."

7

S he jumped up. "You must be joking."

"Please. Sit down and hear me out." He breathed in and straightened up, glad that she slowly took her seat. "I will tell you a bit about myself. I want you to take a decision and whatever you decide, I will accept. My name is Obasse Samuel Edim. I am thirty-two years old. I am a native of Apiapum but I was born in Obubra and I grew up there.

"My father still lives there with my mother. His name is Ovat and he is still a policeman; my mother's name is Nancy and she has a thriving palm oil business. I came to Calabar when I got admission to study Public Policy Administration when I turned 18. I have been here since then."

He didn't take a breath. "After graduating, I worked for two years as a PRO in a private high school before I went for youth service. When I came back, I continued to work for a while as a teacher; for about one year before I decided to work for God. I have been in full time pastoral work for five years now.

"I know my life is very uneventful but I'll gladly answer any question you have." He paused, maintaining eye-contact with her. She defiantly stared back into his eyes, hers betraying no emotion.

"This is a very unusual way of proposing, I know, but it does not really matter as long as there is a conviction. God does not work with facts and figures. He makes way where there seem to be none. This is the conviction I have. Though we just met a few days ago, I can boldly say I know what I am saying." He rambled, refusing to be intimidated by her dour gaze.

"About my family, I am the first of four children from my father though I have a half-sister from my mother. She's about eight years older than I am. She was born to my Mom from a previous marriage. The man died before she met and married my father. I have two junior sisters and a junior brother.

"My senior sister is married to a military man. She has four children. They live in Abuja. Her name is Idik. My immediate junior sister is married also. Her name is Mary. She teaches in a primary school back in Obubra. They have two children. Huh, her husband works in the community bank. He's a banker." He stuttered realising his speech may begin to irritate her. How much of all this information did he think she could assimilate? But he continued undaunted. "My other sister is in the state university, CRUTECH, Akamkpa campus. She's Kwam. And she's twenty-four years. My brother is the last in the family. His name is Okey, twenty–one years old. He just got admission into Unical. He lives with me." He paused, hoping to hear her say something or react. She didn't. He shifted from one leg to the other but continued to stand in front of her.

"My blood group is O+ and I am AA. I don't have any allergies. And I don't have a history of any disease. My salary is from the church. It's not much now but I get a lot of support from the members. I get a basic salary of N25,000.00 with my allowances monthly, I get about N35,000.00. I live with my brother in a two-bedroom flat at federal housing estate.

"Say something," he said suddenly.

She looked at him and laughed. Then she hissed and stood up.

"Don't go without saying something," he said pleadingly. She walked to the door.

"Pamelle," he called and she turned from the entrance, her hand on the doorknob. "Pamelle," he said again softly.

That was when she let out the dam. She began to laugh and she laughed and laughed. She opened the door to his office, and walked out laughing all the way out of the church premises. Her laughter echoed off the empty hall. He slumped into his seat and covered his face.

There was hope. Silence means consent he admonished himself.

8

—·—

The doors of Twins Sights and Tours kept swinging open and closed almost at no interval at all, and when it did once more just before noon, Pam was ready to snap at the customer, to 'go elsewhere.' Her mouth had opened in an 'o' when she looked up from trying to balance the figures, only to widen to a scream! Waning energy surged into her bones and she jumped up to run to her sister.

"Emmauelle!" She shouted, hugging her sister's neck. "Good God! Where did you guys go for so long?" She squeezed until Elle, though also very excited, pushed her aside.

"Pam!" she exclaimed, laughing and choking. "We've been away for just the week!"

"And two days. Mummy is worried sick. Oh my baby!" She followed her sister to slump in the love seat they kept for guests in the howbeit crowded room they ran their business from. She sniffed. "What did that barbarian do to you?"

"Clown." Elle laughed. "How are things generally? Anything happened while I was away?" She looked round excitedly.

YES!

"Nothing much. Just work and more work and plenty of work. I'm ready to drop dead... No. Hand over to you. I'm taking my one week off."

"You dare not," Elle screamed. "In this office, I'm still on honeymoon for the next one month!"

"Yeah right. Yeah right!" Pam laughed. She hugged Elle again.

She'd missed her second so badly. The week had been like a year and they'd not even communicated. After arriving Ghana safely, they'd called to tell everyone they were entering the Bermuda Triangle for a week. Pam had thought it was a joke. It was not possible for Elle not to speak with her in a day. She thought they both couldn't survive it. But it had happened. For a whole week, and two extra days, she'd dialled the Ghana number and gotten stuck with a network clog. That had been very frustrating. She realised she was gradually losing her twin. All their lives, they'd been together and done things together. They had gone everywhere together. Now Elle had a Ghana feather added to her cap.

"Does Mummy know you're back?"

"Yes. I called her. She said she could pop in on her way home today but I don't know if I'll be here by then. Akim wants us to go for dinner somewhere."

Pam winked. "Is three a crowd?"

"If you're the third person, three is a wilderness." Elle laughed. "Have you been making money?" She looked toward Pam's clustered desk.

"More than we made all the time you were here."

"Good. Gives me justification to be married," Elle said jokingly.

"So, how did it go?" Pam batted her eyelids. "Was it painful like they say?"

"Op da! Why did I think I could escape you?" Elle rolled her eyes.

"Because you always were a clown," Pam said. "Tell me everything."

"God, bring customers right now in Jesus' name. Amen!"

"Come, what's your stress? Both of us were hounding Ejiba the other day after her honeymoon..."

"What can I do to escape?" Elle teased.

"You tell me, girl. Every dirty detail."

"You're crazy, Pam. Goodness, it's so good to see you again." She grabbed her sister's neck and hugged her.

"Good try but I still want to hear it."

"Pam, I'm embarrassed." Elle burst into laughter and covered her face. She had never been shy talking to her sister and they told themselves everything all the time. Pam felt a pang of guilt, forcing Elle to talk about her marriage bed, knowing she had a truck-load burden on her mind. But then, Elle didn't know it was there so it was no bother. She knows Elle is no longer a virgin so she justified her insistence.

"Yeah, it was a bit painful at first but oh Pam!" Elle started laughing.

"What?" Pam laughed along.

"I don't know how to describe it. It's like nothing we've ever done."

"Like?"

"Sweet. Nice. I don't know. Your body just feels different. Someone touching you all over, you know?"

"I don't know, God help me," Pam said and they both laughed. It was enough, Pam thought. Things had really changed between them. Elle was now a married woman and no longer the dainty, laughing, mischievous twin they both were.

Well, she initiated the bulk of the mischief and dragged Elle along. They had everything in common but husbands now. Pam had tutored herself every single day Elle was away, that things could no longer be like they were.

The twins had grown up together. There was no place Elle went that Pam did not. They went to the same schools, and did practically the same things. They had exchanged every detail about every date over the years. In university, they had stayed in the same room, though Pam had opted to study accounting because she was good with her figures while Elle studied law. But they'd both agreed to work only for and with themselves.

The Twins Sights and Tours was a one-stop shop for tourists. They arranged vehicles, flights tours and trips, hotel bookings and every tiny detail of touring, including shopping outings and babysitting. Though it was a huge job, they did all from their one-room office at the tourism bureau.

They were lucky to have an office space there at all because the complex was government-owned. When the director of tourism decided to let a private company use the space, the bid had been enormous. But they'd won because of their concept. They were the only company which added 'housekeeping' to their services. And the bureau was a traffic area for tourists.

Their parents had supported them to start the business, furnishing first the office for them. They had hoped to grow. They had a lot of needs. For their business, it wasn't a hit until you could control all your components. They needed cars and buses and more regular staff. The ultimate would be to own their chain of hotels and expand beyond the shores of Calabar.

"Wow. I don't feel like working ever again in my life" Elle was saying. "Can you believe we've not taken one single day off since this place started?" she said. She turned to her side of the office and dropped into her seat. "Goodness me. Let me check my mails. Wow" she switched on her computer and stretched as it booted.

Their dream was a lofty one but Pam was beginning to have a strange feeling it would never be realised. Elle being married and all.

"Well?"

"What?"

"Penny for your thoughts"

"I just missed you so much and I'm just beginning to realise I really have lost you to Akim" Pam said in an uncharacteristic emotional manner.

"Of course not" Elle got up quickly to hug her again. "Oh is it because I said I won't come to work for a month?"

"Of course not" Pam snapped out of her emotions and laughed. "Don't mind me"

"You know I talked about you so much that one day Akim shouted, stop and I didn't even know what he was referring to." Elle laughed.

"You guys were fighting even in your honeymoon?" Pam exclaimed.

"In between stuff" Elle winked and they both laughed. It was so good to see her back. "I know I just came back and we'll still talk a lot but Akim said he'd like to invest in our business" Elle said flippantly.

"Invest in our business? How?" Warning bells went off in Pam's head. She wasn't all that cordial with her brother-in-law. How would she partner with him? When the twins decided to start their business, they never considered bringing anyone in. And Pam wasn't sure now she wanted Akim. He was...

They were just too much alike.

"He wants to pump some money in. If we could buy a few cars... He's offering money to buy about five cars"

"Five cars!" Pam screamed. Half of their income went for car hire.

"I reacted the same way" Elle shrugged, smiling.

"But your husband is such a brute" Pam said lovingly. "He'll come in and turn us both to his office girls"

"I heard that" Akim walked in unceremoniously. Elle jumped up and rushed to hug him, giving him a loud kiss on his mouth. Pam rolled her eyes.

"What are you doing here, honey?" Elle mewed. "I thought you'd pick me up later"

"I was just passing by and couldn't resist taking a look at you"

"Huh! And I thought for a moment you wanted to say hi to me" Pam spat.

"Fangs girl" Akim said, holding Elle leisurely in his arms. "Baby, are you good to go for lunch?" he asked, looking at her sweetly.

"Welcome to you too" Pam pouted.

"Saying it now makes me famished" Elle said. "Is three a crowd?" she looked at Akim.

"With your husband, three is a legion. Thanks but no thanks. I want to work" Pam said. "I've been working on my figures for a while..."

"No need to explain, love. We won't miss you" Akim said sweetly.

"I don't know when you two will ever be nice to one another"

"Don't pray for it, honey. Are you ready?" Akim asked.

"Yeah. Pam dear, I may just pass from lunch to the house. Will I see you later in the evening?"

"Depends on you. I'll go to my father's house after work" Pam shrugged.

"Funny ha ha" Elle smiled. "Akim and I will come and see Mummy in the evening"

"See you then darling" Pam said sweetly, turning back into her seat. "Hey, Akim. Welcome back. Hope your trip was fantastic" she said. They all burst into laughter. But after they left, the smile froze on Pam's face. What now? Everything started playing in her head. All of their twenty-six years had been spent together. They wore the same clothes and went to the same places; did the same things. Pam realised suddenly that over the years, she had come to depend on Elle for everything. Elle was the cool of the two. She could listen forever and give good advice but then she'd met and fallen in love with the notorious heir of the Duke Empire, Akim. And though little changed then, the lat few weeks had been spent preparing for Elle's marriage. No one had noticed how often Akim popped up in their conversation until now. Now Akim could barge into their lovely twin-time and whisk Elle away. She felt so lonely so suddenly. Where would her life go from here?

She picked up her phone and called Osita. She could do with a little distraction. And the guy had called a few times in the past week anyway.

9

— · —

The month passed faster than Pam had expected and she gradually orientated herself with the fact that Elle was not going to be there as she used to be. She could run the office alone anyway and she was very happy for her sister. Elle glowed. Pam had never seen her so happy. Not even after the proposal when she had come out of her quiet shell and displayed enough emotion to last her lifetime. Now she seemed settled and accomplished, and though she had not come into the office regularly, her inputs in the business were quite productive, one of the areas Pam had thought they would experience difficulty. She had sought to discuss Akim's business plan but the successful accountant had been too busy to have a serious meeting with them and Elle could not articulate his intentions.

Pam sat behind her desk and attended to a 'big' customer. It was almost noon and she had been planning on going for lunch, her first meal of the day, at the bureau canteen, when the middle-aged man walked in. He wore a simple striped long-sleeve shirt over stone-wash jeans. But Pam knew not to underestimate anyone in their business. Looks was the number one deceiver in tourism. She had met tourists who wore faded t-shirts and combats, and who spent hundreds of thousands of naira, without being able to speak one single word in English!

"I am organizing a tour of the state for elder statesmen from all over the country" the man said, after introducing himself as Commodore. Pam opened a fresh page on her daily planner diary and made notes. "So far, I have sixty-five of them who have confirmed they'll come. All together, we hope to bring hundred"

"Please give me the full details" Pam said.

"They'll come in on a Friday morning. We hope to move them round by road in Calabar and then they spend the night here. On Saturday, we hit the road and sleep at the Obudu Ranch Resort. They spend the whole day Sunday at the ranch. Monday, we drive back to Calabar. They leave town Tuesday morning"

"Do you want us to take care of all the details? Transportation, hotels, food, shopping et.c."

"Well, I guess" Commodore sighed. "We are bringing them in from all over the country so some of them will come by air, others by road. What we are going to do is work with different agencies to bring them here. You will have to take over from here".

"When is the tour?"

"We have two months to the date. You do know that most of them are septuagenarians. Their care is very important to this tour. Can you arrange it?" he asked hesitantly.

"Definitely"

"I did not expect to meet such a young person" he said. Just as Elle walked in, looking ruffled.

"You have nothing to worry about" Pam said quickly. "Please meet my partner and twin" she said. "Elle Duke. Meet Commodore"

"Oh hello" Elle said, half-dazed. Pam knew something was wrong but it just had to wait.

"Commodore is organising a tour for elder statesmen from all over the country. I believe you'll have women also?" she looked at Commodore inquisitively.

"A few, yes"

"I'll need to know the figures exactly. Can you get that for me in the next few weeks?"

"Definitely"

"The way we operate is very simple. We give you the actual cost of the package. You have to pay 50% of this upfront. Along with the service charge of 20%. On arrival, you'll have to pay the full charge" Pam said, seeing Elle lean against the wall from her blind view. "We also charge 5% VAT"

"I'll need the figures as soon as I let you know how many of them are coming" Commodore said, still not very convinced.

"We have a track record, Commodore. You'll be surprised how professional our services are" Elle said, leaning forward. It was a good deal. She would not want them to lose it.

"Until I see your charges" Commodore stood up.

"We'll definitely be in touch with you" Pam stood up and extended her hand. He shook her hand briefly and then Elle's.

"I have your card" he said as though to remind himself. Pam thought she would contact him first. She was sure he would visit one or two other agencies to compare.

"So what's..." Pam started after Commodore had left.

"You need to help me, please, Pam" Elle said quickly.

"Yes? You look like you're just coming from a war front"

"I'm just coming from the market. Akim called that his pastor was sick and I should cook for him. But then I just remembered I had an appointment with my doctor. I have to go for it. Can you help me do the cooking? Pam, please. I ..."

"Wait a minute. Calm down. What are you saying? I should lock up the office to cook for your pastor? Are you kidding? It's ten in the morning. Work just started!"

"But Alice can stay in the office while you're away. See, I have everything in the car. I'll drop you at his house and you can just cook. Akim said he's very sick and..."

"What time is your appointment?"

"Eleven!"

"Why do you need to see a doctor anyway? Are you sick?"

"I missed my period" Elle said.

"Oh"

"Oh?"

"Oh, yes. Great! Wow, sis" Pam hugged Elle. "So what's this about the pastor? Must it be you?"

"Well, I agreed without thinking"

"What do you want to cook?"

"Draw soup and fufu" Elle said. "It won't take long. The pastor is very sick"

"Alright, let's go. I won't want to be away for more than an hour" Pam said reluctantly. Alice was one of the office assistants in the bureau and usually helped them with some typing. And other times like this, when both had to leave the office.

"I'll just call Alice while you pack" Elle hurried out. Pam smiled. Elle pregnant? That would be great. The excitement surged through her. She would be an aunt. She picked her bag and looked around her table for anything she needed to pick. Grabbing the keys, she walked out and locked the office. She met with Elle in the bureau main office and after thanking Alice sincerely, they left.

"Where's your pastor's house?" Pam asked casually.

"Federal Housing Estate" Elle said and manoeuvred the 2000 model Nissan Sunny Akim had given her as a wedding gift out of the bureau complex and entered the highway.

A resounded bell clanged in Pam's head. He had said he lived in Federal Housing with his brother. No. It had better not be that pastor. She shifted in her seat. How would she know and what would she do even if she did know? She had made up her mind not to tell her sister a thing about what happened in Obasse's office that night. Though she continued to question her decision each time she saw her sister, the decision had stayed. She wished for a second that she hadn't. She wasn't the secretive type. Her words came out of her mouth as soon as they were formed in her mind but somehow, she couldn't bring herself to talk about this. Probably she would not be heading to his house now if she'd told Elle about it. But then she wasn't even sure it was him.

"Doesn't he have a wife?"

"No"

"What's wrong with the pastor exactly?"

"Malaria. Akim said he sounded like he was dying when he called him. His brother who stays with him travelled a few days ago and when the illness came, he thought he could cope"

"So why didn't he call someone else? Why you and your husband?" Pam knew now. He was the one. Well, she would keep to her code. Hear no evil, speak no evil.

"Actually Akim had called him. He said he hadn't spoken to him since we got back and he felt guilty but when he spoke with him, he saw the man didn't sound right. It was after probing, he got the details"

"Oh, it is not your church pastor?" Pam feigned.

"No. It's Pastor Obasse, the one that preached at our wedding. He's no longer in the parish"

"Oh, I see. The looker"

"Ah, Pam" Elle laughed. "The man is not bad o" Yeah right, Pam thought. Wait till I tell you what he did to me. If I do tell you, that is.

"I'm so happy for you Elle. About your baby" Pam said brightly, changing the subject.

"Well, we don't know yet" Elle replied.

"What do you mean by that? It must be"

"Amen. It's so soon after the wedding. I didn't expect it" Elle shrugged. Pam burst into laughter.

"You know what? You pretend too much. What did you expect? To be barren?" Pam scolded. "This is just formality. Get ready to push" Pam laughed.

"Ee yah" Elle smiled.

She turned into a fenced compound and packed the car close to the fence.

"Here we are" she said cheerfully. "He stays at the flat behind"

Here I am, Pam thought glumly.

10

The house itself looked small and choked. Pam assumed it must have been improvised from a one-bedroom flat to two. Howbeit, it was neat and smelled clean. The blue and grey curtains on opposite sides of the small sitting area were not drawn and the house was a bit dark when they entered. Elle had simply knocked and opened the door.

"Don't they lock their door?" Pam asked surprised.

"I don't know" Elle shrugged.

The furniture in the room was sparse with three single cane chairs and a wooden centre table. A rather nice dining set was pushed against the north wall with four chairs. A ceiling fan hung idly over them. Elle looked for the switch and turned it on, then off, then on.

"No light" she hissed. She moved to draw the curtains, bringing in a little illumination. "Let me find him" she said to Pam who stood flaccidly in the middle of the room. Such a humble living, she thought.

"Pastor" Elle called moving into a dark passage. There was a low reply from another room. "Pam, come" she said.

"I'll find the kitchen" Pam said and moved to another door beside the dining. She opened it to a small but neat kitchen. In one glance she saw the table-top refrigerator, the kerosene stove, with a groan, and the neatly stacked pots and crockery on the kitchen table. There was adequate work space on the table and she placed the ingredients Elle had bought from the market on it. The stainless steel sink was clean and clear. She opened the tap and clean portable water gushed out.

"Thank goodness" she muttered. Unpacking the bag, she found everything she needed to make a sumptuous *ogbono* soup, with fresh vegetable leaves, dry and stock fish in abundance, the ground ogbono itself with crayfish and fresh beef; and already made fufu which she knew Elle must have taken from their mother's refridgerator . She immediately set about cooking the meal. She had roughly one hour here.

"He's in the room, drowsy but I told him I couldn't stay. I have to get to the hospital. I'll come back after the appointment" Elle said, coming into the small kitchen.

"Don't worry. I'll get back to the office on my own" Pam said, cutting the meat into small chewable cubes.

"Are you sure?"

"Yeah. Of course"

Elle blew her air a quick kiss and hurried out. She was running late for the doctor's appointment. Pam leaned forward over the meat and sighed heavily. What a blast? She had thought she could forget all about the occurrence of that night. She had refused to admit it happened, laughing it off as a dream. Why would she be in his kitchen cooking for him? It was a very bad joke. Yet she hadn't been able to tell Elle. And she had hoped she would not meet him again, for crying out loud, he wasn't even Akim and Elle's pastor anymore.

Well, she would cook and leave the food on the table for him. She didn't need to see him. After the food is ready, all she needed to do was call out to him she was leaving. What if he came to stay with her while she cooked, she thought suddenly. No. He was sick. He would not come and stand and hound her. With that resolve, she set about doing her work. Ogbono was one of the easiest soups to cook, and she was a specialist in it. Aptly, she shredded the vegetable leaf, steamed the meat till it was quite soft and added the ingredients. While the soup cooked, she mixed the home-made fufu and turned it till it was a smooth paste. As soon as the soup was done, she put the fufu on the fire and turned it till it was soft and smooth. The one made at home was always nicer than the commercial one and their mother had taught them never to buy. The normal odour that came with fufu was absent in this one. Elle had chosen a nice meal for a sick person.

Once the food was done, Pam cleaned up the kitchen, putting away the remaining ingredients, some in the fridge and the rest in a food cupboard she discovered behind the kitchen door. She dished the food in two plates and covered it, placing it on the table with a bowl of washing water, a glass cup and cold drinking water she removed from the fridge.

"Pastor" she called from the parlour. There was a grunt from the direction of his room. "I've finished. The food is on your table and I'm leaving" she said blandly.

"Alright" he murmured inaudibly. "Thank you very much. God bless you" he said. She headed towards the door and stopped. He did not come out. Heaving a heavy guilt-laden sigh, she turned back. After all, he was a human being. If he was someone else, she would have checked on him. Besides, Elle would ask her if he ate or not, whether it was her business or not, and she would not want to say she left without even seeing him. That would be callous.

"Can I come in?" she asked at the entrance of the room.

"Yes please" he mumbled from under a blanket. The room was hot and stuffy. The curtain was drawn and the windows were almost all shut.

"How are you?" she asked, standing at the edge of the king-size bed.

"Ok. Thanks." He said. He looked really sick.

"You don't look ok." She moved to the head of the bed and bent over him, touching his forehead gingerly. He was scorching hot. "You're very hot. You shouldn't cover up like this with such a hot temperature" she said, pulling back the blanket. He tried to hold it back to himself. Under the thick cover, he wore a long-sleeved shirt and black trousers.

"No, I'm cold, please" he shivered. She straightened and opened the windows fully. Then pulled the blanket away completely and folded it at the foot of the bed. He curled up.

"You need fresh air. Have you had your bath?" she asked. Why didn't Elle do all this anyway?

"No. I can't stand up"

"You have to" she insisted. "Here, let me help you up" she tugged on his arm and he leaned heavily on her. They staggered together and he straightened, leaning against the wall.

"Use lukewarm water, and leave the water on your body, don't dry yourself" she said. He nodded and walked slowly to the adjoining bathroom. She pulled the sheet off the bed shaking it thoroughly before spreading it back. Then she switched on the fan, hissing elaborately when she realised the electricity was still out. She busied herself by tidying the room while the shower ran. When he came out of the bathroom, wearing the shirt and trousers again, he was trying to control his shivering.

"I had to use cold water, no light to heat it a little"

"Do you have any light clothing, like a kaftan or pyjamas?" she asked.

"I have pyjamas" he said.

"Don't dry your body. Wear the pyjamas and I'll wait for you in the parlour" she commanded and marched out of the room. Her head was pounding when he finally came out staggering. What was she doing here? She wondered wearily. He wore a nice and clean purple striped pyjama.

"I made fufu and draw soup for you. And you have to eat" she said, sitting at the table. "Come here" she said. He walked to the table and sat like an obedient sheep. "Try and eat". He looked at the food and shook his head. His breathing was fast. It was obvious he was very weak, but struggling to be strong. She remembered what he said about faith talks. "Ok. I know what I'll do." She dipped her right hand in the washing basin swiftly. "I'll feed you" she said. She'd just fixed her nails the day before and hated eating with her fingers but there was no other way to get him to eat. She cut a small morsel of the fufu and dipped it in the soup, and stretched it out to him. That was when he looked into her face. His eyes dark and wanting, his breathing quickened.

"Eat" she said. He opened his mouth slowly and she put the food in his mouth. Inside his mouth was almost as hot as his body but when he shivered, it wasn't because of the fever. There was another fever catching up on them both. He held her gaze, unable to look away. When she withdrew her hand from his mouth, a small dollop of soup trickled down and involuntarily, she licked it off her fingers. A deep groan arose from his chest and he closed his eyes. She swallowed hard, wondering where all her raging feelings were coming from.

Determinedly, she cut another piece and gave to him. "Eat" she urged in a whisper. She made sure he got everything in his mouth this time. Quietly, she cut the fufu, rolled it in soup, and put in his mouth. He received it and licked her fingers. It was quite a small mound she had dished for him, and he finished it.

"That's very good" she said, packing the plates.

"I want more" he said, looking into her eyes. She had a strange feeling it wasn't the fufu he wanted. He had licked her finger clean when she placed the last morsel in his mouth.

"You'll be nauseated" she said. "I see you're getting better already" she teased. She cleared the table and came back to him. "Try and eat in the evening. When is your brother coming back?"

"I've sent for him. I started getting sick the day he left, three days ago. He should come in this evening"

"Have you taken any drugs?" she asked before thinking that he was a pastor. "Or you have faith?"

"Medicine is one of the gifts of healing. I took some anti-malaria drugs yesterday"

"You should rest then, and don't cover yourself up. You need fresh air"

"Thank you" he murmured.

"If you need anything call someone. Don't just hole up in here and kill yourself" she chided softly. He nodded. "Bye and take care of yourself." She picked her handbag and walked out without looking back.

He walked into his room and looked through a window that gave a perfect view of the frontage. She stood for a minute to catch her breath and then turned to look at the house. He hid behind the curtain to conceal himself from her view. She was obviously disconcerted. What had happened in there to them? He had never felt so intimate with anyone in his life, except probably his mother. A funny thought came to his mind and he half-smiled. When Elle had come to check on him, he had not felt like seeing anyone or doing anything. And he had told her so, almost rudely. And then Pam had come in and he had done everything from taking his bath to eating like a new-born baby. When he looked back to the front of the house, she was walking away. Probably as shocked as he had been. He felt well suddenly. In fact, he felt like ten men. Oh God bless Akim for telling his wife about this sickness. And God bless his wife for telling her sister. And God bless her sister for being such a sweet angel. And God bless God for being God. He sighed and went back to lie on his freshly made bed, leaving the blanket exactly where Pam had left it.

11

Elle returned later in the day to the office with the good news. She was pregnant! Pam screamed and made a lot of noise and they hugged and kissed themselves. Pam was about to close the office so they locked up together. They went out to take a drink together and talked about the doctor's report. It was too soon to say anything apart from that she was pregnant but she was going to be closely monitored.

"So how did the cooking go?" Elle asked abruptly. "I called Pastor Obasse and he said his brother had arrived"

"Cooking went well" Pam said sharply.

"I'm sorry darling. I know how you hate to cook with kerosene stove" Elle said. Oh! Good excuse, Pam thought. She hadn't minded cooking with *his* stove. Whatever happened afterwards was her main concern; and the only reason why she didn't want to talk about the whole experience.

"Too late now, isn't it?" Pam shrugged.

"He was a bit agitated on the phone too..." Elle paused, and Pam held her breath before her sister shrugged. "He's sick anyway, and the network was bad". Pam shrugged again. He had been agitated, she wanted to ask why. She really didn't want to talk about this! What happened to the gist of the new baby?

"Well, he was very grateful for the food. He said his brother gobbled half of the pot of soup when he arrived"

"So the saying goes" Pam answered.

"He said..."

"So, what sex are you expecting? I want a puff-pooh little baby girl" Pam cut in suddenly.

"Akim wants a son. An heir to his throne!" Elle laughed, unable to resist the new topic though surprised at the abrupt change.

"Please. After the first girl, he can have six sons if he wishes" Pam dismissed.

"And who will be the mother of those boys? Not me. I'm stopping after three"

"The average" Pam teased. "In quick succession I hope"

"Hmm. What about you? Osita says he wants to visit you" Elle goaded.

"I can't remember anyone asking him not to" Pam said in sweetness.

"You like him, don't you?" Elle laughed playfully.

"Well, he's not bad. He has some bucks. He's good looking..."

"Is his money an issue?" Elle exclaimed.

"Excuse me! Are you the only one who should marry a millionaire?" Pam rolled her eyes. "He's coming" Trust Elle to have told him where to pick them up. She'd known that would happen when she came back to the office in a taxi.

"Who?" Elle turned just in time to see her husband. He looked worn out with his jacket flung over his shoulder.

"Are you girls ready?" he asked, bending to give Elle a peck on her cheek.

"Yes" Elle replied breathlessly.

"Congratulations, I hear it's a girl" Pam said, oblivious of Elle's blinking and eye signals to stop her.

"A girl? You've got the results?! Oh my God!!" Akim scooped Elle up from her seat and hugged her tight. "You didn't tell me, honey girl" he kissed her face.

"I wanted it to be a surprise. Silly Pam can't keep her mouth shut" Elle replied. "And we're not sure it's a girl yet, don't mind her"

"Oops, sorry" Pam dodged from invisible assault.

"We have to celebrate this..."

"That's why we came for a drink. And I'm on my way home" Pam said, standing up.

"Who wanted to involve you in the first place" Akim asked.

"Do I get a drop or I should start trekking"

"Trek"

"Come on"

They all walked out of the eatery where Elle and Pam had chosen to have a drink. The couple dropped Pam off at her mother's house and drove off into the night without coming in to say hello. Pam shook her head and watched them leave. They were such a bubbly happy couple though Pam had not thought they could be. Their courtship had caused Elle a lot of heartache because of the kind of person Akim was – ruthless, arrogant, proud. Pam had hated him at first sight but he made Elle very happy. And that was the most important.

"Are you going to stand there forever?" Mummy's voice came to her from just inside the house and she turned away with a sigh, to walk into the house.

It wasn't late yet but their mother was already dressed in her nightgown and housecoat.

"You won't stop missing her for a while. At least not till you get married" Mummy said. "Welcome. How was your day?" she asked. No-go area, Pam thought. As in, how the day was.

"Fine, thank you. Good evening, Mummy" Pam greeted.

"I thought Elle would come in" Mummy said disappointedly.

"Akim was driving. They want to rush off to celebrate" Pam said cheerfully.

"What are they celebrating?"

"Elle is pregnant! You're going to be a grandma!" she yelled and hugged her mother.

"Eh! Eh God, thank you o! Is that why they couldn't just come in to tell me?"

"They're too excited. Akim just heard about it this evening. I don't know what your daughter was planning but I let the cat out of the bag so he insisted they had to go and celebrate somewhere"

"Oh thank God. God has finally given me comfort from your daddy's death. Hmm"

"Oh Mummy, you'll start now and make us both cry to bed. This is a happy day" she sighed. "I'm going in if you don't mind. I am tired"

"Aren't you eating? Beatrice cooked rice before leaving".

"No, I'm too tired to eat" Pam said, suddenly feeling a warm tingle along her right fingers. The sensation of someone licking her fingers had remained with her since it happened. She'd even washed her hands again after she returned to the office but the feeling remained. Beatrice was a day staff they had employed to help with cooking and cleaning around the house, just before their father died, and after the tragedy, she had become almost like a nurse to the twins and their mother.

"Beatrice said she added some oxtail to the stew especially for you" Mummy tried to encourage her. She loved oxtail. It was the only thing she enjoyed eating with her hand, till this afternoon. Seemed Fufu and Ogbono soup had been added.

"No, Mummy. Maybe I'll take it tomorrow" she said.

"Are you alright?" Mummy asked, worried. Pam never rejected an offer like that.

"Yes. Really," she laughed. She didn't feel alright. She had emotional fever, and she was running temperature... emotionally. It started after she left Obasse's house. Her mother squeezed her face and she shrugged. "Okay. Just to prove to you I'm very fine. I'll have some" she dropped her handbag on the sofa and trudged to the kitchen. The smell of the stew alone made her heap her plate with some boiled white rice and a healthy portion of oxtail. Mummy sat across from her and watched her eat. She didn't bother asking because she knew their mother never ate any time later than six in the evening. It was part of her health and diet plan.

"Is it because Elle is pregnant?" Mummy asked suddenly, shocking Pam. At first her mouth popped opened, almost spilling meat in her mouth, and then she laughed.

"Of course not, Mummy!" Pam yelped. "I am so happy for Elle. I was worried she won't be happy with that Akim!"

"Then what is wrong. You're not yourself. You're not even eating this food with... spirit" Mummy said.

"Eh o, Mummy! I don't understand you o! I'm enjoying this food. I am so alright" she lied.

"I don't want you to compare yourself with your sister. I tell you that all the time. You may be twins and look alike but you are two different people with different lives to live. Are you hearing me?" Mummy said insistently.

"Yes ma!" Pam saluted.

"You may think I am joking but I am not. God forbid my children will fight because of jealousy..."

"Mummy, please. I don't like that. I am not jealous of my sister. I am very happy for her. I am happy. How can you say that?" Pam cut off the playfulness.

"I'm not saying you are jealous, I just don't want..."

"I know. It's okay" she snapped and continued eating in silence.

"Well, I mean no offence. I love you very much"

"I love you too, Mummy". She finished her food and stood up hastily. Now she was very upset. Coupled with the fever. She just wanted to go to her room and sleep it off. "Good night, Mummy".

"Don't you want to watch TV? It seems they'll show a very interesting movie tonight" Mummy said, feeling bad.

"No, you watch alone tonight. I want to sleep" she hugged her mother quickly and left for her room. She couldn't get into her night dress and into bed fast enough. She hugged herself under the covering wrapper and tried to block such feelings as she had out of her mind. For goodness sake, all the odds were against him.

He was a pastor! She never wanted to be a pastor's wife. He didn't have money! N35,000.00 a month! That was ridiculous for a university graduate. She sometimes made more than that in a day in her business. On a rare day, anyway, but not in a whole month!! He had a family load of responsibilities as the first son. If they got married, where would his brother stay? In that rat hole with them? She turned away and scolded herself. She had decided not to think about it. She would not.

She wrapped her cover wrapper over her head and repeated again and again that she would not think about it. Most importantly, she had sworn not to marry from her village or tribe. What happened to all the Ibo and Yoruba and Yala men for crying out loud! Even Elle who was not particular about tribe or tongue got a nice, rich Efik man. And he was old. Thirty-two? No way. What would she be doing with a frail thirty-two year old man? When he is eighty, she'll be baby-sitting him even though she's just six years younger. She'd rather marry someone her age than marry a thirty-two year old! Akim was thirty. And she had chided Elle that he was old. She had the image of a twenty-eight year old, rich doctor or something in mind. Someone handsome, she could show off. Even Osita was much more qualified at thirty. A pastor! What future does a pastor have apart from making heaven? They would be transferred from church to church, meeting all sorts of people who thought they had a right to the pastor's very existence. She hated the way people treated their pastors. They would come into their homes and disregard the pastor, and get away with it. Because he is a pastor! Pastors were everybody's foot mat. He ensures you're clean but you leave him dirty! The pastor's wife takes all the shit rubbed off the pastor. No way!

If she married a pastor, she would chase away all the parishioners from her house. They would hate her and leave the church.

No. It was a joke that the only man who'd ever asked for her hand in marriage was a pastor. It was God's way of cracking a joke.

12

—·—

P am stood outside at the parking lot and waved at the departing group. Thank God, that was that. The school children from out of town had occupied her every minute in the last few days and she thanked the God of heaven for granting them an uneventful stay. The twenty-five kids, aged between 10 and 15 years had driven over 400kilometres from Benin City on a tour of Cross River State. Pam had arranged all the visits for them, as soon as they arrived Calabar. They had visited the Tinapa Business Resort and spent the night at the hotel there. The following morning, they'd driven through the length of Cross River State to the Ranch Resort where they spent two nights before returning to Calabar, passing through Kwa Falls. They'd visited the museum early on the last day before hitting the road at about 10a.m. It had been gruelling and she felt she deserved a day off work. But Elle had started having funny feelings. She told her it was in her mind because the so-called morning sickness had begun the very next day after the doctor's report. That was a week ago. She had to keep the office open, and she had to do her tours. Another group was due to arrive from the Northern city of Kaduna the following day, and they were staying a week! What was that saying about looking for work and getting the work!

She had swung back towards the office wearily first and then she stopped short and turned back. She had noticed the tall figure passing through the gate just instinctively seconds before it registered in her mind. Pastor Obasse was walking towards her with an anxious look on his face. Well, why not? She hadn't heard from him since the day he decided to give her a sleepless night. Not even a call to say thank you. But why would he? He'd told Elle the thank you, and she'd told her. That was enough!

"Pamelle" he greeted. She hated being called Pamelle. It sounded like pummel. And she did a lot of it in school and when she was growing up; for herself, and for her sister. When the kids wanted to upset her, they called her pummel. It drove her crazy.

"Good morning, Pastor Obasse" she greeted politely.

"I called Ella and she told me you were here" he said.

"Her name is Elle. Not Ella" she said rudely. He looked at her undaunted.

"Elle, sorry. I keep thinking she's Emmanuella"

"No, she's not" she replied sharply. It had irritated her when he kept calling her Ella on her wedding day! He stood for a moment staring at her.

"May I come into your office?" he finally asked.

"I thought you were not going to stay long" she said. And he smiled disarmingly. He had a lovely smile, she'd noticed. His smile alone may have won her heart.

"I intend to stay long with you" he said brutishly. His meaning was not lost on her and she was rankled by it. She swung on her heel and matched to her office. He followed quietly. Her office was a mess. She had not been inside for two days and obviously Elle had not had either the mind or the strength to tidy it up. She wanted to apologise for the untidiness but caught her tongue. Who cares? She didn't ask him to sit either. There were magazines on the visitor's couch and he pushed them away, inviting himself to sit.

"Your ogbono made headlines in my family" he said casually, throwing her off balance. Her mouth popped open to comment and she shut it right back, extracting laughter from him. "Thank you. I needed to come and deliver this personally" he said.

"It was one of those things" she muttered.

"My mother came with my brother. She finished off where you started from"

"I didn't start anything"

"She just wanted to know exactly who cooked that soup" he said conversationally, refusing to acknowledge the scowl on her face.

"And you told her your member's wife, I guess"

"I told her the twin to my former member's wife" he said, and she squeezed her face. "Her expression exactly. So I had to explain in detail. Including how you fed me!"

"That is not funny" she whispered.

"She wants to meet you" he said.

"No way. If that's why you came here then please leave. I will not meet your mother for any reason" she blew up.

"Hey, she went back home the following day. I just came to thank you"

His cool answer unnerved her and she went to sit behind her desk, unsure of how to treat him. He was as relaxed as she was tense. She clasped and unclasped her hands on her table.

"Well, Elle thanked me for you and that was enough" her tone had a conclusive lilt.

"I've been thinking of how to repay you..."

"It's not necessary. I did it for my sister" she said.

"It's not nice when you snap and interrupt someone. It doesn't make you like pretty!"

"Excuse me" she flew to her feet. "I don't want to be nice or pretty to you. You can leave my office, thank you" she said angrily.

"You can't send me away until I am done here" he said with a low voice.

"This is my office and I can ask you to leave" she said. He looked up at her then and into her angry face, and stood up.

"You almost made me forget to tell you. Your outfit is lovely" he said softly. It deposed her, and she looked at herself involuntarily. She wore a black chinos skinny twirl trouser with pink cutwork shirt. It was very comfortable on her and she hadn't given it a second thought until now.

"Thank you" she said stiffly.

"I'll be on my way" he said, moving towards the door. She stood rigidly, fuming for no reason, apart from that he had come and was now leaving. At the entrance, he turned back.

"I don't know if you want to hear this but I'm going for a program somewhere and I thought you may want to come with me, if you're free tonight" he said.

Okay. This was the actual reason he came she thought angrily. This is exactly why she would never marry a pastor. Instead of taking you out to dinner, they take you to *a program*! How so romantic! She sniffed.

"Okay" she found herself saying.

"Thank you" he smiled. "Here's the address" he scribbled on a piece of paper he picked from his shirt pocket quickly and handed it to her. "Time is 6pm"

"Okay" she said again, now angrier with herself than him. Why? She should throw the paper in his face and tell him off.

"I'll see you in the evening" he said and walked through the door.

She looked at the paper in her hand. Sumeez hall was not very far from her house. She could close from work a little earlier and go home to change.

For what? A voice screamed in her head. It was bad enough she had dumbly accepted his invite. She should tear the paper and forget he came but she couldn't. He was so nice despite her rudeness, which he didn't deserve anyway. Why was she so angry with him? He had never been impolite or nasty to her, yet she was always nervous around him. Maybe it's because of the way he was looking at me at Elle's wedding. I hate people looking at me, she said to herself. She pushed the sheet of paper into her front pocket and went back to work. The office was a mess and she would not want any other visitor to come in and find it so dirty.

She was ashamed already that his first time in her office, and the place was so filthy.

13

S umeez hall, a multi-purpose hall cum church, was packed to the fullest when she arrived at 6pm on the dot. She walked through the gate and stood awkwardly aside, wondering what she was to do next. Was she to wait for him? Should she enter and look for a seat? She wasn't even sure what kind of meeting it was. As she stood listlessly, an usher approached her, smiling.

"Do you want to go in and get a seat?" he asked. She turned to reply and saw him alighting from a commercial motorcycle.

"No, thanks. I'm waiting for someone" she said, goose bumps suddenly emerging on her body. She shivered as though cold as he reached her side. The usher smiled and excused them.

"Thanks for coming. You look lovely" he said. She didn't look any lovelier than when he saw her in her office. She had only changed her shoes from the pink pumps she wore to the office to black strap high sandals. In fact, she felt musty and work-weary. She had brushed her long hair back in a hurry and repacked it with her hair ruffle without checking it in a mirror. And she had refused to retouch her make-up despite the fact that she had struggled with it. Her total look was not bad, but definitely not lovely. Did he just tell lies compulsively? She wondered. He looked lovely on the other hand in a fine tailored black suit with linen striped shirt, buttoned to his throat. He wore no tie. She hated ties anyway! What happened to cravats?

"Let's go in" he said. She nodded and followed him. He passed through the crowd and headed for the front of the hall. She was shocked when an usher collected his Bible from him and ushered them forward. Someone she assumed was the host of the program hugged and shook him gladly. She stood uncomfortably and waited out the greeting and then he turned to her and over the noise of the praise worship made introductions.

"Please meet my good friend, Pastor Jasper. Pamelle Ukpabi" he said. She smiled stiffly and nodded, ignoring the pastor's outstretched hand. The pastor smiled and greeted her warmly. She felt so out of place. Obasse sat down and motioned for her to sit beside him.

"Please God knows I'll kill you if you ask me to greet the church" she whispered in his ear as she settled down.

"I wouldn't dare" he whispered back teasingly. "I don't want to die yet" and he smiled that winning smile at her. She frowned.

Apparently the service had started a while before they came in. The loudness and vibrancy of the praise gradually gave way to solemn worship. The worship leader was a young man with a sweet tenor voice and his music brought the heavens close. Pastor Jasper climbed the altar and the singing gradually stopped. He went into a short session of prayer, after which he introduced Obasse elaborately.

Obasse climbed the altar and hugged his friend as he collected the cordless microphone from his hand. He lifted his hand up and started a worship song in a sweet deep voice. The tenor brother raised it up for him and the whole church joined in. Pam loved the song: You are the reason I live; and she sang from her heart, getting caught up in the flow. The atmosphere suddenly became very tense and Obasse called out excitedly.

"God is visiting with His people, worship Him" he shouted. "Worship the Almighty. He is so beautiful for every situation right now. I see angels in this place, pouring out oil on the heads of the saints, oh Halleluyah". The worship leader took another song: Great is your mercy towards me; and the congregation went up in a loud roar. Obasse lifted up his hands towards the heaven and sang in worship. It was impossible not to worship. Several of the members shouted words of prayers in unknown tongues. Some went on their knees, weeping like children. Others just stood with tears dripping down their faces unbidden. Pam bent over with her face covered mumbling words over prayer. It was not possible for anyone to stare. Obasse lay flat on his face crying. The tenor boy took the song: I see the Lord; softly. A loud scream rent the air and a young lady fell backwards, causing a string of confusion along the column.

"Oh thank you, Jesus" Obasse stood up slowly. "Do what only you can do. Move in this place tonight Lord. Halleluyah!" He walked the length and breath of the altar and came down to the pews, moving round and worshipping God. "God wants to do something special here tonight. Release yourself. Free your mind. The Holy Spirit is touching people around here." He stopped in front of the row where the young lady had fallen down and looked at some of the expectant faces. "God wants to touch someone here" he said. Another lady fell forward and two men fell back into their seats. Obasse walked back to the front of the hall and looked at Pastor Jasper. "Do I have liberty of the spirit here, brother?" he asked. Pastor Jasper nodded eagerly.

"I don't know if I can preach here tonight. Holy Spirit, please take over" Obasse said. People continued to sing, some following the song leader, others singing and praying on their own. It would have been rowdy and noisy but the sweetness made it different. People fell without being touched by anyone around, someone forward, some backwards, some rolled on the floor, sweeping chairs and making waves, others just wept. A lady shook as though very cold, another was sweating profusely. One man ran to the front of the hall shouting 'fire, fire, holy ghost'. Obasse went back to stand on the pulpit and prayed quietly. Gradually, there was calm.

"If you know something happened to you tonight, come forward" Obasse said. "God is telling me there are at least fifteen people here who received instant healing. Come out and testify"

People rushed forward.

"If you were healed, stand to my right. If you just felt a touch, stand to my left" he said. The crowd separated. Obasse invited Pastor Jasper to come and assist him and they prayed for the people on the left first. Almost all the people fell down as the two pastors prayed for them. Ushers rushed to help the fall, laying people down as they lost control of their legs. Pam noticed the ushers were having a hard time catching the people and she moved forward to help.

"Thank you, my friend" Obasse nodded at Pastor Jasper, who went back to his seat. He moved to stand in front of the people who had received healing. "I want you to tell me what God did for you in a moment" he said, giving his microphone to the first person, a man.

"Pastor, I came here tonight with acute stomach pain. I could not bend or stand straight but then I felt warmth all over me as you prayed. I don't feel the pain any more" he said, laughing.

"Halleluyah, church! Glory to Jesus. Do those things you couldn't do before" he replied. The man jumped, bent, straightened, and laughed.

"I couldn't laugh without feeling pain, pastor" he said, suddenly close to tears.

"How long has the pain been there?"

"Since this afternoon."

"Your healing is complete, in Jesus' name" Obasse laid his hand on his head lightly. The man shouted and fell flat on his back. An usher had missed catching him by a breath. Pam rushed to stand behind the next person.

For the next thirty minutes, over twenty people testified of various healings ranging from headache and migraine to other less visible pains. Obasse prayed and laid hands on each of them, before they went back to their seats. When the people had all gone back to their seats, Obasse offered a prayer of thanksgiving and preached a very short message on the spirit of truth.

The meeting closed almost two and a half hours after they arrived. Obasse thanked Pastor Jasper profusely. His friend handed an envelope to him in appreciation.

"Thank you very much, Pastor Obasse" Jasper said.

"I thank God" Obasse said, excusing himself and Pam. They walked out amidst the throng of people going back home while Jasper talked with some of his leaders in the church.

"It will be hard to get a bike with this crowd" Pam said softly.

"Let's walk to the main road" Obasse replied.

They walked quietly to the main road.

"There's a nice suya spot here. I thought you'll like to take something?" he asked, already leading the way down the road.

"I should be getting back home" she excused.

"It won't take long. And I promise you'll like the suya" he said, imploring her.

"Doesn't look like I have a choice" she shrugged.

"Thank you" he replied. He got a nice space for them at the suya spot and then stood up to place the order for the suya and drinks at the spit. She smiled to herself. Was this a date of sorts? Program and suya? Huh, very funny. She thought. But after that powerful ministration, she had expected he would not talk normally again. Hmm. The inside life of a pastor beyond the pulpit. It sounded like a good movie title. She had never been close to her pastors though her parents had brought them up in the church. They had always held their parish priest in very high esteem. Though Rev. Uka had four children, it had never crossed her mind that he did the basal things other human beings did to have a family. How funny, she smiled.

"I'll pay to know what brought that sweet smile to your face" he said, coming to sit opposite her, and placing two bottles of soft drinks on the table between them.

"How much?" she asked.

"Name your price"

"That's big faith, pastor. Knowing how much you earn!"

"You'll be surprised" he winked.

"Ten grand"

"Hah hah! Wait till end of the month then" he laughed. She joined in. "So what was funny"

"Private girly thoughts" she said.

"I should receive a word of knowledge to bring it out"

"Funny ha ha!" She picked her bottle of drink and sipped slowly with the straw.

"Thanks for helping with the ushers tonight" he said, also taking his drink.

"Hmm. I've never done anything like it before. I was so scared those people falling would harm themselves"

"That's the mystery of the Holy Spirit. It's amazing. Some fall so hard and yet feel nothing when they get up. I guess you've never fallen under the anointing before?" he asked.

"Never! And don't bother yourself with my opinion about it"

"What's your opinion? You don't believe it's real? You feel we push people down?"

"I have had only one similar experience" she started. "I went on invitation to a friend's church. The man, or pastor called me out and I was impressed he said some accurate stuff about me. Then he laid his hand on my head and started praying. He prayed and prayed and bent my neck till I thought it would snap. He turned it to the right and to the left. When I realised he would not give, I stepped back, freeing my neck. He came on to me again and this time I went on my knees. That was when his prayer finished."

Obasse laughed so hard, it made her laugh.

"My friend was so embarrassed. I told her I will never come to her church again!" Pam said, laughing. "Huh. Is it by force?"

"But it doesn't always happen that way. Some people really do get the touch"

"After tonight though, I think I'll like to know what it's like" she shrugged. His head swell up and he felt like ten men. "Holy Spirit really moved for you tonight" she said.

"Thank Holy Spirit" he said gladly.

"Rev. Uka never does any of those things. You know we orthodox prefer the old method of worship" she said. "But we receive the Holy Spirit and some of us do speak in tongues"

"It does not reduce the efficacy of your worship of God. I know Rev. Uka from way back; he's one of our mentors in ministry"

"Exactly. I like that. Many of you vibrant evangelicals believe only your people will go to heaven" she said.

"It's foolishness to think that. After I met your pastor about eight years ago, my impression about orthodox churches changed"

"Halla lu jah!" she said. He laughed.

He excused himself to collect the suya and they spent the rest of the evening chatting about everything from church doctrines to sports and politics.

"Can I ask a personal question?" he asked, looking at her over the rim of his glass.

"I'll only answer if I like. But ask" she said.

"If you won't answer it, then I should not embarrass myself by asking" he replied.

"Ask" she said firmly.

"How many men ... how many men have you loved before?"

"None of your business" she exclaimed.

"That tells me one thing, either they're too numerous to count or none" he said. "So which is it?"

"My sister and I grew up in the church, and we are not hypocrites. So choose whichever you like" she smiled to her drink, wondering why he would want to know. She thought of throwing back the question to him but then, he would gladly reply and that would set them on another course.

"None. You have never been with a man" he said. He looked into her eyes. "You're a virgin" he whispered, feeling indescribable joy.

"Don't take that to the market with you" she said. "It won't sell"

"The truth's hard to sell to people who are blind to it."

She shrugged. "Thanks for keeping yourself" he added.

"Please. Talk about something else" she looked away shyly and he laughed, embarrassing her more.

"I did not keep myself and that's one of my greatest regrets. I respect you" he said solemnly.

"Thank you". She itched for details but could not bring herself round to it. How many women had he been with? He started talking about the temptations that surround young people and how passionate he was about fighting it; casually drifting away from the 'personal' topic.

When he checked his watch at almost eleven in the night, he blew a whistle, and ensured he saw her to her doorstep before turning to go back home, his head in the clouds.

14

—·—

Holiday periods were particularly hectic for their kind of business. The tourism bureau in addition to being a one-stop shop was organising a state-wide symposium and the office had all sorts of people roaming in and out, missing their way and all. Elle stood up from her seat and stretched after redirecting a bunch of non-English-speaking French men to Alice's office. The weather that morning was bright and promising and though it was still more than an hour before noon, the offices were quieting down with the lunch hour lull. The first few work hours had found them bustling with unending activity, and they'd only just enjoyed a few moments of calm.

"Akim will be travelling today and I need to get him ready for the trip" she said, subconsciously rubbing her stomach. It was still as flat as it had always been but Elle was as conscious of the baby as though her belly was bulging. Pam looked up from her the weekly report she was preparing on the computer.

"Is it today?" she asked in wonder.

"Yeah. And I'm going to miss him like air" Elle sighed.

"I don't know why you're not going with him. You'll just be so boring here. I know you'll talk about missing him every second of the day" Pam said, resuming her work.

"He also asked me to follow him but I was thinking about you"

"Me? Don't be silly. Five days will not kill me. Anyway, you haven't been around much. So, don't lay it on me, girl"

"I've always wanted to visit Jos and this would have been so nice" Elle moaned "but Akim is going to be in the seminar from morning till evening"

"And you can get a taxi to drive you round the city during the day. Anytime you're tired you come back" Pam encouraged.

"Are you sure you'll be alright alone? See how busy the office has been these last few days" Elle looked at her sister longingly.

"Don't even think about me" Pam made a comic face briefly.

"Let me call him" Elle said excitedly. She made a call briefly and sighed. "He'll pick me on his way home. His driver will drop the car back" she smiled uncertainly.

"What?" Pam stopped and looked at her.

"Will the baby be alright? I haven't flown since this pregnancy and they always said it affects the baby sometimes" she said worriedly.

"Are you sick?" Pam asked concerned.

"No. I'm just worried"

"You can ask Mummy. I'm sure she'll know, cos I don't" Pam shrugged.

"Yeah. Let me start preparing" she sat up and started to clear her desk.

"Did Akim say anything about his interest in this business again?" Pam asked suddenly. "I keep forgetting to ask you"

"Yes, but not in detail yet. He said we need a car for the business" Elle looked at her face in the office mirror and rubbed powder on it.

"It'll be good to know what he has in mind so we know how to move on"

"He's even thinking also of leaving it totally to you to run. He thinks I'm under stress"

"Tsk" Pam snickered.

"God forgive you" Elle laughed.

"If I do all the work, I'll get all the dough, baby. No qualms"

"I have to go, he's flashing me" Elle said. She rushed to her sister and gave her a peck.

"Call me when you get to Jos"

"If I decide to go, that is" Elle rushed out, calling a quick, Bye. Pam shook her head and continued her work.

By noon, Pam was truly tired. She stood up from her almost-finished report and went to the canteen to have a quick meal. People were milling all around the bureau, most of them curious visitors and tourists. It was good for their business anyway, but very stressful. The canteen was an improvised office with tables and chairs and it was usually choked up during lunch time. Pam managed to find a just-vacated seat and placed her order for rice and stew. She had a lot of work to do especially with records. She had neglected her order of reports and had a pile waiting to be updated.

She was half-way through the meal when she looked up and almost choked on her food. Osita stood smiling at her.

"What on earth?" she laughed. The other three seats on her table were occupied by busy eaters. She stood up and hugged him. "No one told me you were coming today!"

"How are you?" he asked, smiling. "I came in last night but wanted to surprise you today" he said.

"I'm going to twist Akim's neck. I'm sure he knows you're here"

"Elle too. But I hear they're travelling to Jos today"

"I'll pinch them both" she said cheerfully. "What brings you to Calabar?" she asked, turning round the table to stand with him.

"No, finish your food" he said.

"You think I still have appetite for it? No way. Come on" she said. She led the way to the counter and paid for the food, leading him back to her office. "What brings you to Calabar?" she asked again as she opened the door.

"Business. I have a partner here we've been discussing for months about a new venture we want to go into" he said.

"What sort of business?" she asked.

"Well, some kind of ur, retailing, we haven't yet formalised it" he shrugged.

"What's the product?"

"Hmm, we're still working on the packaging" he replied evasively. "So what have you been up to?" he asked briskly, looking over her office as they entered.

"Nothing much" she shrugged. His elusion of the topic of his business did not miss her. She hated when people dodged questions. Why don't you just say you don't want to talk about it yet because there are still a lot of issues to be...?

"I said your office is nice" he interrupted her thoughts.

"We're not there yet but..." she shrugged stiffly. "I guess you're not sure of when you'll be leaving town?" she asked rather sharply.

"On the contrary, I'll be leaving tomorrow morning. We have another meeting in Abuja."

"Nice. Do you want to eat or drink anything?" she sat down as he looked at some of the tourism shots pasted on the wall.

"No, I just had some snacks before coming here. I'm actually in the middle of a meeting. I wasn't sure I'd be able to see you after the meeting. We may close late" he said.

"Oh. That's so nice of you" she said. What else did one say to someone so stuck-up? "For coming, really. I would have loved to entertain you" she said.

"How about dinner then?" he asked.

"Do you know when your meeting will end?"

"Huh, I'm not sure. We may be staying so late" his regret seemed plastic. Why did he come here? Probably Elle had implored him! So much like her.

"Don't you worry about it. I'm really glad you could make time out of your tight schedule" she was dismissing him. He would have none of it; he sat down and picked one of the magazines and started talking about tourism prospects in the state.

When he finally took his leave about half an hour later, saying he was really late but did not regret the sacrifice of visiting her; she started to breathe again.

The day moved on very fast after that. She closed as soon as she had a free moment from clients and enquirers and took a bike to Obasse's church. There was no weekly service but he had asked her to come over after work. Whatever for. She had again assured herself it was not necessary to keep him in her thoughts. She didn't mind being his friend, and that was all she would allow between them. His new parish was bigger than the other one and situated on a main street. The offices were located at the back of the auditorium and she walked the length through neat rows of more than six hundred plastic chairs. He had told her his office was to the left of the hall, close to the altar. She found it easily and knocked before opening the door. He was talking to another man of about his age.

"Good evening" she greeted.

"Oh welcome" he said cheerfully. The man nodded at her coolly. "Have a seat." He pulled a seat over for her, seeming very excited. "Let me introduce my assistant to you, Pastor John. Pamelle Ukpabi" he turned to the pastor. She quickly thought of asking him to call her Pam as soon as they were alone.

"Pleased to meet you" John extended his hand to her and she took it.

"Thank you" she said.

"I'll come back to finish the ..."

"Oh not at all" Obasse said quickly. "It's alright for Pam to be here"

Pam! Did you just say Pam?

"I can wait outside" she said, standing up quickly, making for the door.

"Of course not. Please make yourself comfortable. We won't take long" Obasse said quickly. Pam's mouth formed an 'o' and she shrugged. Pastor John wrinkled his nose in disapproval but Pam ignored him.

"So as I was saying, the accounts of the church have to be handled properly. Suspicion of theft is rated as high as theft to me" Obasse said.

"Sure, Pastor" John said, looking over his shoulder at Pam. She sat with her knees together, her hands clasped on them like a young school girl waiting to be reprimanded. "I understand that perfectly. Pastor Ubong was a stickler for details before he retired"

"The books don't show it much" Obasse said. Pam stood up, aware of the tension between the two pastors and looked at a small crammed bookshelf standing against the wall. She looked at the books for a while and then started to arrange the books, effectively blocking out the strained conversation the men were having. She was almost through with neatly arranging the books alphabetically when Pastor John's voice jolted her to their presence.

"We hope to see more of you?" he asked, looking at her carelessly.

"I guess" she mumbled.

He walked out of the office without another word and Obasse came to stand beside her.

"You look really beautiful in that outfit" he said. She subconsciously looked at the white gipsy skirt and red wrap-round blouse she wore and smiled.

"I think not. I think you just say that all the time without really looking at me" she remarked.

"That's not fair, because it's not true. Believe me anytime I tell you something" he sulked.

"Yes sir" she saluted.

"You're a very beautiful woman"

"Tsk"

"I see you're giving my office a make-over?" he teased.

"I like neatness, especially in the office" she pushed the last few books into place. Straightening up, she looked at the quizzical expression on his face. "Don't think because you saw my office in a mess, it means anything" she laughed.

"I haven't said a thing" he raised his hand up and laughed.

"Your assistant didn't like discussing issues with a stranger around" she rebuked.

"You're a stranger to him, not me. He'll soon realise you're not a stranger at all"

"Don't go there"

15

It actually started like a small joke which she didn't find funny. Then he started negotiating, tasking her even. He went as far as offering her a fee before she angrily accepted to do it, free of charge. There were several reasons why she was reluctant. First, she would see him every day till she finished because she would work in his office; it was part of the deal. She didn't like that. She would rather reduce the familiarity developing between them. Secondly, his office environment was not work-friendly. His assistant was not friendly either. His office was stuffy and small and there were a lot of interruptions; what with the office tripling as the church library and store. The third reason was purely selfish. She wanted her time after work to herself. She had a right to her own life and privacy, something she suspected Obasse was trying to merge with his own.

But despite the odds, she accepted grudgingly to audit the church account for him. In over ten years since the establishment of this big parish, the accounts had never been audited not internally, or externally. Pam found a jumble. The more she tried to categorise the accounts, the more she found new and strange entries. Once she found an entry that stated, pastor's lunch. Then several pastor. Pastor.

Pastor.

She ended up creating a category for pastor's sundry expenses. Then there was church sundry expenses. Welfare sundry expenses. Then there was pastor's miscellaneous welfare expenses and another pastor's wife.

Pastor's wife.

"People are just collecting money from this church account anyhow" she told him after a long gruelling third day. "I have entries for pastor, his wife and John". They were in his office again and she had packed the records as she had them properly stored in his file cabinet, under lock and key.

"That's why I hired you to do this for me" he smiled. "Will dinner be appropriate ..."

"No, please. I'm tired and I want to go home"

"Tomorrow night then?"

"I want to finish this before I start my life normally again" she said. He chuckled. "I've finished putting in all the entries. I already have to create a new account for just miscellaneous. Anyway, you'll see it when I finish"

"Thank you so much" he said seriously. "I don't know how I'll repay you"

"I'm just wondering though; John does not like this at all. And you've been here for just a couple of weeks and you're making all these changes..." she shrugged.

"It's just enquiries. No changes yet. I like my accounts to be straight. When I asked for the accounts records, I was shocked when they brought all sorts to me, small note books, even sheets of paper. No proper documentation of anything" he explained.

"It indicts the former pastor"

"He was a very good pastor and I don't plan to indict him. But I like my books to be straight from the beginning" he shrugged.

"Ok" she hummed. The accounts were really in a mess. More than half of the monthly income she realised ended up between three people: the pastor, his wife and Pastor John, who at the time was the church administrator. The assistant pastor to the former pastor had been taken to head another parish, and John elevated to the position of the assistant pastor, while a new administrator was employed.

"I've been thinking, you know, this account thing has set me really thinking" she started, eager to share her thoughts with him. "Your pastors are very poorly paid. And not too poorly anyway, because you hardly do more than praying and preaching" she stared at him. It sounded like an insult in his ears.

"What do you mean?" he croaked.

"I mean no offence and you may not want to hear this" she shrugged and stood up to stretch.

"You're not going till you finish what you have to say" he demanded softly.

"What do you do during the day?" she asked sharply.

"I pray, I study, I counsel" he replied defensively.

"Not much to lay men like me. And probably we determine your salary?" she shrugged.

"The church board determines pastors' salaries" he said.

"And what are the professions of the church board members?" she asked, irritating him.

"I don't know. Lay men like you, I guess. Doctors, lawyers, accountants, business men and women. What is your point?"

"My point pastor, is that lay men think they work harder than you do. They pay tithes and offerings and think pastor does nothing but counsel preach and study and so should not be paid anything nice. After all, parishioners will still bring token gifts to the pastor" she explained.

"Yeah, so? I get a lot of gifts sometimes. If I work hard, praying, preaching, studying and counselling, people come and appreciate me. That's how it works"

"My point is, what you are paid is commensurate to the way you are valued. For you, your monthly value in the sight of your board members is 25 grand." It was like a dirty slap in his face. He looked away from her insistent face angrily. All because he told her his salary?

"That's why all the stealing goes on" she landed the heavy one.

"Who's stealing?" he turned on her.

"There's a lot of expenditure that does not fit! You see a lot of pastor's lunch. Pastor's wife entertainment. Suit for pastor. This or that. And honourarium! What on earth is honourarium? I had to create an entry for it because it was so large. Ten thousand, fifteen thousand. Even fifty thousand! I even saw one or two as high as hundred thousand!" she exclaimed.

"Honourarium is a gift given to guest ministers when they come to preach"

"OK" she mumbled, nodding slowly. "Just like what your friend Jasper pressed into your hand the other day" she said jeeringly. "How much was in the envelope?"

"Ten thousand"

Her eyebrows rose. "I was wondering what was in it and why"

"A labourer is worthy of his hire. It is appreciation of the gift on a man's life" he said stiffly.

"But why so much? Honorarium in your church is as high as four hundred thousand a month on the average!"

"Is that what you call stealing?" he bit out softly. He wondered why it was so high also but he couldn't bring himself to admit it.

She matched to the cabinet and pulled out the account files again. She flipped through numerous sheets of paper and stood straight to look at him, holding one loose sheet in her hand.

"This is the record for July. As of two months ago, your church recorded one million and twenty five thousand for tithes. Total offerings and sundry pledges, thanksgiving and children's offerings amount to eight hundred thousand and some change." She looked through more sheets and brought out another single page. "Recorded expenses states that the tithe of total income sent to your headquarters was one hundred and twenty thousand naira. The difference of sixty two thousand plus is non-existence. That is what I call stealing" she said snugly. It annoyed him extremely. Was he to regret involving her? "I think you should get a chartered auditor to do a more thorough job" she put the sheets back in the file and started to put them away.

"How dare you, Pamelle? I can't believe you'll use privileged information to make mockery of men of God" he burst out.

She was shocked by his outburst but immediately put the file away and turned on him.

"Excuse me? Who asked for your privileged information? Can you just imagine?"

"I just don't like the sound of..." he started softly but she was fuming. She picked her bag and matched towards the door. He stood up to block her exit.

"I don't care what you like or do not like. I should never have involved myself with you or your church" she stood in front of him. "Get out of my way"

"I'll not allow you to be rude to me" he snapped. "You're not leaving till I'm ready to leave with you. And that means when we finish this conversation"

She pushed him aside with force, knocking him off balance, and opened the door. Her angry steps rang down the church hall. Obasse straightened up slowly, breathing hard to calm himself. He contemplated following her only once and made up his mind.

She was at the entrance when his voice reached her.

"Akim calls you Pepper because of your behaviour, is it not true? If you think I'll allow you to be rude and nasty to me, you've got another think coming" he shouted. It produced the desired effect. She stopped short and turned round as he moved slowly towards her. "They say you are the container, beautiful and all, but you've got no content. You're rude, nasty, selfish and proud. And you think I'm not good enough for you?" he said as he approached her. She stood too shocked to speak.

"Elle is the content; epitome of womanhood, a delight to every man. You think you're the son your parents didn't have and you try to behave like one? All you try to do is sniff a little of that pepper you're completely made of in every one's eyes."

He stood in front of her as she twitched her eyes and jaws in controlled explosion.

"You think I'm not good enough for you?" he whispered in her face. She raised her hand to slap him but he caught her wrist just in time and pulled her into a tight embrace.

"How dare you?" she tried to struggle. "Let go of me! Leave me!!"

He held her to his body stiffly, suddenly struggling to control an arousal he had not expected. She was too close. He could feel her body from shoulder to knees.

"I'm sorry" he whispered in her ears. "Don't leave alone"

She shoved hard and he stepped back, releasing her. "Don't leave alone" he repeated.

She marched into the night.

16

She didn't show up in his office for two days. The following day, she sat fuming in her office. How could he talk to her like that? What did he think she was? She wasn't one of those ninny-livered so-called girls that worship the very ground the pastor walked on. She had seen too many of them during her campus days. It was one of the reasons she stuck to her old-fashioned orthodox church. Good old Methodist! They loved God more than most of these Pentecostals. On campus she saw her course mates calling their contemporaries 'daddy' and 'mama'. It was one of the most foolish things she has ever seen manifested. Yet, she could not understand it. Some were even older than their 'daddies' and 'mamas'. Respect, she thought. Manipulation, more like it. She could not dispute there was something about being a clergy anyway. She could see herself fighting it with Obasse also. Fighting that 'fear' that is such an air around God's servants. Fear that they would pronounce a curse on you, and that would be the end. And yet she still could not understand why a man of God like Obasse, or any man of God at that, would find her attractive, enough to propose marriage to. She was 'worldly' in simple terms. Even Elle told her so often.

Elle was the pastor's wife material. She was calm, loving, and patient. Pam was the exact opposite.

Part of her anger with him was that he'd been right. She never cared about rubbing pepper in people's eyes. Now she expected him to tell her he was no longer interested and that he would want to recall his proposal. But she had refused to pick his calls throughout the day. If he wanted to talk to her, he knew where to find her.

The day after that, he sent a text begging her. She didn't want him to beg. She wanted him to leave her. But she had missed him the day before. She forced herself not to go to the church after her closing hours. Instead she went to the suya spot and treated herself to a lonely snack.

But then, on the third day after their quarrel, she closed early and went to his office. She had shunned him for two days. She only excused that since he wanted her to finish with the accounts; she had committed herself to that. She only had to balance the entries. All the unaccounted funds, she had lumped into the miscellaneous entry. And it was an unconventional miscellaneous entry. No auditor will leave it unqueried. The honourarium was another bothersome entry.

His office was open but empty when she got there. A very bad sign. There were some scattered books from the shelf she had so painstakingly arranged the previous week, on the shelf and around. She shook her head, annoyed. No respect for this pastor's office, she thought. If she were to have her way, the library and store would be moved to a general office or any other place. But she couldn't have her way.

She sat on the visitor's chair across from his own and waited for him to come. She was sure he would be around some place. His Bible was opened on his table and it seemed he had been preparing for a message of some sort. She felt a pang of guilt about her comment on the pastor not working hard. It wasn't easy to be a pastor. On preaching, and praying, it may not be a hard job, but on counselling, it was hard. The pastor carried the guilt and pain of everyone else on his head. He was supposed to rejoice with his members in their happy times even if he was passing through hell in his own life; and vice versa, he was expected to mourn with a mourning parishioner, even if his wife just delivered their first son! Like the doctor, the pastor was meant to set aside his own feelings and attend to his members, and he was on call all the time.

The door opened and she automatically looked up. A lady walked in. She was dressed for church even though Pam knew it wasn't a meeting day; in a modest, floral blouse and black skirt. Her nylon scarf was tied tightly round her head. She looked at Pam hideously. Her face was passionless, like those by sculptor graved for niches in a temple. Pam gave her a once-over and continued flipping through the new novel she had picked up out of boredom the day before. The lady would have been pretty, but her face was naked. She wore tiny stud earrings and a thin costume gold chain hung around her neck. She wore black, peep-toe high sandals.

"Who are you?" she asked.

"Pardon?" Pam looked up at her again.

"Is that some sort of greeting?" the lady snapped. "Who are you and what are you doing in Pastor's office?" she snapped.

"What are you doing in Obasse's office? Remind me if you greeted or not? You met me here, did you not?" Pam hissed. Oh God, why had she even bothered to come?

"What insult?" she started just as Obasse walked in. He smiled pleasantly at Pam and looked at the lady.

"Hi, Sister Atai. Is it time yet?" he glanced at his watch. Pam stood up abruptly. "Are you leaving?" he gasped.

"Obviously pastor, you have a guest and I'm not about to sit in while you discuss with your *guest*" Pam replied.

"Did someone upset you?" he asked as he took his seat.

"Pastor, please may I take a seat?" Atai asked sweetly, taking the only other empty chair in the office.

"Pam, sit down, I won't be a minute" he said, looking at her. She sighed.

"I'll come back tomorrow..."

"Here, take the key to the cabinet" he removed it from his pocket quickly and dangled it in front of her. She sighed again and collected it reluctantly.

"Pastor, who is this? And will you allow her to be inside here while we talk?" Atai asked in horror.

"Is there something private you wanted to talk about?" Obasse arched his brow in surprise.

"Yes" Atai said firmly.

"I'm surprised. You didn't sound like that when you called" he said easily. Pam walked to the cabinet and brought out the files. She drew her chair towards the shelf and backed them.

"Tell her to go away, Pastor" Atai insisted.

"I'll not be able to do that. When I have visitors, she turns deaf ears. Believe me" Obasse said, almost playfully.

"Well, Pastor. I came to tell you that I am now ready" Atai said sluggishly.

"That's a wonderful idea. Is that what you call private?" Obasse smiled. "I'm really glad about that. Why, are you not happy?"

"I'm very happy for the relationship. I took time to seek God's face, and now I'm convinced. I came to tell you we can fix a date now" she said, staring blandly into his face. Pam worked as quiet as a nun breathless with adoration.

"Fix a date for what?"

"Our wedding. Or do you have other plans for me?"

"Atai, is this why you came here or am I missing something?"

"I knew you'll not want to talk about such important plans under the circumstances. I'll come to your house" she stood up.

"No, wait. Don't come to my house" he stood up but she was already at the door.

"I understand" she blew him a noisy kiss and strolled out. Obasse was shaking angrily.

"Atai, come back here... Is this girl mad or something?"

"Don't bother." Pam mumbled. "She'll see you in your house later" she laughed and hissed.

"That's not funny. That girl is a little girl. Just one silly little girl. I don't even know what she was talking about?" he defended heatedly.

"Why would she be so bold to talk to you like that if she's a little girl?" Pam turned to look at him. She was shocked to discover within herself that she was not joking any more.

"I don't know, Pamelle, really..."

"Stop calling me Pamelle, I hate it!" she snapped.

"I'm sorry" he burst out.

"She said she was ready. Ready for what else? Did you propose to her? How many of us did you propose to?" she fired. She wished to calm down and blinked to see if he was actually smiling.

"You're jealous" he said softly.

"For what?" she shouted. "What am I jealous over? Anybody can come here and say what they like!" She felt jealous. It was just because she hated been short-circuited. She wished she had told him off immediately and turned down his proposal. Now it seemed as though two of them were contesting for him. She hated any type of contest, especially if it was over a man. She never fought for a man. If they were two of them, she stepped down.

"I have never asked any other woman to be my wife, except you" he looked at her seriously. "And while I am still expecting a reply from you, I can never ask anyone..."

"Don't expect a reply from me!"

"Atai and her mother came to me last year asking for help. Her mother had been a very committed member of the church but Atai came only a few times. She only got committed after counselling her. At that time however, Atai had been delinquent. She was not ready to re-sit for her final exams which she'd failed several times. She was not ready to learn a trade or do anything. She had a silly boyfriend who got her pregnant. So I told her she should go and have her child. When she was ready, she should let me know and we can talk about what she would do next. She called me about an hour ago that she was coming to see me. I didn't know this is what she was coming to do.

This is so mischievous. I had always suspected she had a mental challenge of some sort. Honestly" he looked at her intently.

"Come on, Pam. Look at her. I couldn't fall for her even if I tried!" he said. It brought abrupt laughter from her and she felt ashamed for her fury. "Thank God, Pam, you're laughing with me again. I was so scared you'll never come here again"

"That girl must be up to some mischief. Does she know me?" Pam asked.

"I'm so surprised. I see all sorts of people in this my life and job. I think she goes crazy every once in a while. If I'd known she was high I would not have asked her to come. She's not even a member of this church. Her mother attends my former parish" he drew up the seat Atai just vacated and sat beside her.

"I'm sorry for saying all those terrible things to you" he said quietly.

"I was just trying to help, I didn't mean to be rude" she replied. "You were right anyway"

"No ... I had no right..."

"No, I had no right." She felt very light apologising to him. She hardly ever did. To anyone. "I'm sorry too" she whispered.

"You don't have to apologise for anything. I'm grateful to you for what you're doing"

"I was rude. Please accept the apology" she insisted.

"Ok." He looked at her and their eyes connected for a moment before she awkwardly looked away. To think she almost slapped him a few days ago! That would have been terrible, she thought. "So, what else have you discovered from the accounts" he asked changing the subject and reducing the tension between them.

"Nothing after what I told you. I'm worried for you, though"

"What about?"

"This investigation you're doing"

"Don't worry about it. I'm not going to take any action on it. It will only guide me to direct the accounts"

"That's why I'm worried. You should take action on it. This is criminal. You should report it. Some of the months where honorarium was as high as five hundred thousand naira, there are no records of any special programmes. Who got the honorarium? Or is honourarium for the parish pastors and local speakers too? As in, local within the church? Say, the assistant pastor preaches, you know?"

"I understand what you're saying and the answer is no. We don't give local speakers honorarium" he slouched, dejected. "If I report this to headquarters, someone's going to be very mad with me..."

"That's if it's a *someone* and not some people"

"Exactly. I may be in serious trouble, persecution and so on. And if the person not happy with me is my superior, it may affect my calling" he groaned.

"Takes me directly to my point. I've been studying you know, about pastors and men of God in the Bible. Some of them had other means of living, some temporarily, some permanently. Like Paul, did tent-making for some time to sustain himself"

"I vowed my whole life will be devoted to the service of God" he shook his head adamantly. Not ready to hear of it. "I will never take up secular work again"

"I don't mean that. There are ways of making money by the side. You could invest in stocks and ..."

"I don't have the kind of money to invest in stocks" he stood up and rubbed his temple. He was beginning to have a headache.

"There are short-term stocks and bonds…"

"God is able to provide for my needs" he maintained.

"If you report this and they start to persecute you, throw you around, suspend your salary, what will you fall back on?" she asked.

It was a good question but one he wasn't ready to answer.

"I don't know. I don't know I want to report it"

"Then get a professional auditor or ask your head office to send an auditor"

"While I was in the other parish, auditors came annually" he said thoughtfully. "They should have come here also"

"Unless John blocked them on the way and stuffed them with honorarium" Pam stated.

"That's a grave allegation."

"You have to do something about it" she insisted. "It's your duty as a pastor to stand on the truth" she argued.

17

—·—

The Saturday morning was bright and beautiful, beneath a sky as fair as summer flowers. A kind of day you wanted to get married. The bride wore a beautiful white damask skirt suit, unusual for such an occasion, and a white veiled hat. The groom was just as unusual in a white damask Italian cut suit, and white cravat. Obasse officiated the wedding. Pam loved the couple's outfit badly. She couldn't stop talking about the wedding long after it was over. The weather was beautiful; the couple was beautiful; everything was just so beautiful. Pam was in a gay mood. She laughed and joked at the reception with the people who sat on her table; Obasse, John and Jasper.

After the event, Obasse encouraged her to follow him back to his house to spend the rest of the day but she refused. Ever since Elle got back from Jos with Akim, she hadn't spent any sensible time with them and she wanted to visit them. She left the men at the venue of the reception. The other two men followed Jasper who had volunteered to drop them off at the church since Obasse decided he would rather return there.

"Who is she?" Jasper asked in the car as he skilfully manoeuvred his red Audi 80 out of the premises of University of Calabar Hotel where the reception had held.

"My friend" Obasse replied.

"You came with her to the programme at my church. I was going to ask you but it kept skipping my mind" Jasper said. "Just a friend?" he asked quizzically.

"A very close friend, Pastor Jasper. She doesn't attend the church but she's there everyday" John said tartly.

"That sounds like an accusation. I hope the man of God is still in the spirit?" Jasper asked.

"Yeah, she's quite close. But what do you men really want to know? If she's my wife or what?" Obasse asked, chuckling.

"That will be ridiculous. She's not even born again" John said.

"How would you know that?"

"Look at her. See the way she dresses. Short, sleeveless dresses, tight jeans, low-neck tops; and even look at the way she treats everybody in church." John said heatedly. Obasse turned in his seat to look back at him.

"How does she treat everybody?" Obasse asked calmly.

"As if her father built that church. She's so arrogant and rude" John added. Obasse grew uncomfortable.

"Seems there's hostility here" Jasper said. "You're not aware?" he asked his friend.

Obasse straightened in his seat. "I'm hearing this for the first time" he shrugged. "Pam never gave me an inkling of any problem"

"Oh, Pastor, so she did not tell you she's been having problems with church members. See?" John hissed. "The other day she insulted the ushers sweeping the church when she came in. She told them to go to hell!"

"Nobody told me" Obasse looked quite harried. It wasn't unlike what she could do. He knew there would be a reason for it anyway but she never spoke about it.

"Hmm. I was just waiting for a right time to talk to you about her. She called Festus and told him to move the store and library from your office."

Obasse turned back in shock to look at his assistant.

"She does things in that church o. She comes round when you're not around and questions people. She asked Mma Rose how much her salary is and told her that it was too much, there will be a cut. That girl, Pastor. Let me not talk" John said, looking directly at Obasse.

"People just keep quiet because she's always in your office and you're always happy with her" John retorted.

"You'd better look into these allegations, Obasse" Jasper advised sharply. "This kind of thing can scatter your church"

Obasse was too surprised to comment and these were things he couldn't defend Pam about.

"Especially since she's not a member of the church. And if she's not a believer, hmm. I don't need to tell you it's not right for her to be seen with you like that"

They got to the church, Obasse still dumbfounded.

"I'll see you later" he waved at Jasper. He needed to talk to Pam so badly.

"You can ask the chief usher because it was reported to him" John said as they walked into Obasse's office. "Even me, she's been questioning me. My wife is even aware"

"Pastor John, thank you. She's my friend and I trust her so all this is new. I'll know what I'm going to do about it" Obasse replied softly.

"In fact, the other day, I don't know what she came to do in your office and…"

"Pastor John, I want to prepare for tomorrow, if you don't mind" Obasse smiled, and closed his door in his assistant's face before the latter could protest. He sat at his desk and could not do anything. His head was pounding. It was early evening; Pam would be with her sister. He pulled out from his drawer the report she'd prepared for him. It had been two weeks since the report was given to him. It was painted red! There was no way he would submit this report and not be in the bad books of several of his superiors. Every single one of the ten-page annual financial report spelt 'theft'. The pastors had been stealing from the coffers of the church. Yet Pam had told him he must expose the truth. How could he sweep such an evil under the carpet? One thing was sure, if this report was accepted, John was in deep trouble. He had been contemplating calling him and discussing the report but would that not be conspiratorial. Yet, this man worked with him. If he sent such dirt to the senior pastors without talking to him first, would that not resemble a betrayal? He pondered his many options. It was right to report without bias. Already, he had put a structure of accountability in place. Every single monies received was accounted for but the rottenness was there. John now did not handle church funds and had never done anything to incriminate himself. But.

And it was a big but.

What about cleansing the system? The former pastor had retired to go into full-time evangelistic work. What if he had repented? Reporting would dig up buried and forgiven secrets. And what was this sudden issue about Pam? She had consistently asked him about what he would do. But John had been suspicious, he knew. Several times he had burst into his office under one form of pretence or the other when Pam was there. Pam had confessed to him that she had no love lost for John, and she felt the feeling was mutual. But the occasions John sited could be corroborated.

He needed to talk to her first.

He called her number and she picked it up after the first ring. There was laughter in the background. It was the joy he didn't feel right now.

"Are you still with Elle?" he asked the obvious.

"Yes. Where are you?" she asked, her mouth making a noisy eating sound.

"In my office" he said.

"You didn't go home again?"

"No"

"Are you alright?" she paused.

"I want to see you"

"Are you okay?" This time there was a hint of anxiety in her voice. He felt guilty for judging her without hearing her side. "Should I come over?" she asked.

"No" he breathed in. John was still around. He would not want him to know that he had decided to talk to her first before talking to at least one of the members he'd referred to.

"Can you come to my house?" he thought it was a bad idea. It was getting late. But he didn't want to go to Elle's house or her house. Her mother would be there. He sighed. His house was the best bet. His brother would serve as the chaperon.

"Okay. I'm coming" she said and hung up before he could say anything more. He figured she would take a while before she got there. He tidied his desk, and kept the report back under the lock of his drawer.

John jumped back when he opened the door.

"Are you leaving, Pastor?" he asked nervously.

"Yes. Did you want to see me?"

"Not really, I was coming to tell you that I'm leaving also"

Obasse had a funny feeling it was a lie. Whatever. He had no cause to question John as a minister of God. He was loyal. He was committed. He attended every meeting in the church punctually. In short, he was a model minister. He was married with a daughter and he had never given Obasse cause to suspect him of any shady behaviour with women in church or outside. His wife was the president of the women's fellowship and he had never had reason to settle any problems in the women's fellowship. There was nothing wrong with John, aside from what the finance records had revealed. And he could well shut his eyes off it since he was not the pastor at the time.

Exactly what Pam had said he would be held responsible for if he did.

18

—·—

She was sitting in his parlour when he arrived. She looked at him critically when he entered, looking for any signs. He noticed she had changed from the dress she wore to the wedding, a very nice baby blue georgette lace skirt and blouse. Now she wore a yellow drop-waist embroidered dress. The neck was low and he took a deep breath before looking away to compose himself. No matter what she wore, it always had the same effect on him.

"Sorry, I didn't leave the office immediately" he said. She stood up then "Sit down" he croaked, taking another seat.

"Is something wrong?" she asked.

"Where's Okey? Why didn't he offer you something to drink?" he asked looking around.

"He should be around. I told him I didn't want to drink anything" she replied impatiently. He turned back to look at her. His expression was grave. She was so beautiful it took extra courage to challenge her. He tried not to sound judgemental but when he finally spoke, it was obvious whose side he was on.

"What's been going on between you and the church members?" he asked.

"What church members? Going on how?"

"Don't pretend with me, Pam. I hate it. Is it true you've been insulting ushers, and staff of the church?"

"Insulting ushers?" she questioned.

"You know the meaning of that English word, don't you?"

"Ahha? What sort of query is this?" she slowly became irritated. "If there's something you want to say, why don't you just say it?"

"My assistant pastor, Pastor John said you've been asking people what their salaries are around church. You've been rude to ushers, and to him; and you treat people with disdain in the church. In his words, as though your father built this church! Is it true?"

Emotions flashed across her face like the sweep of sun-rent clouds over a quiet landscape. Shock, then red-hot anger.

"Your assistant pastor, the rogue? What are you telling me here? Is this why you brought me rushing from my sister's lovely company to your house? Pastor Obasse, are you alright at all?" she flew to her feet.

"Sit down, right now, Pam" he barked. Like a cold wind his words went through her flesh. She sat down more out of an unexpected fear than from obedience. He stood up, struggling to control a fury he could not understand.

"Now listen to me carefully" he said with a calm he did not feel. "I want to know every single correspondence you've had with any one in that church behind my back. This is not the time to be smart or funny or angry with me, because I am very angry with you, right now. I'm listening" he sat back and leaned his head over the edge of the chair, staring at the ceiling. His posture annoyed her more than his order. She contemplated her reaction. If she stomped away, it was likely he would follow her. She decided at once to answer his demand and never have anything to do with him again in her life.

"I'll take your claims one at a time. I have never had any encounter pleasant or otherwise with any of the ushers apart from the few times I come for service and I sit exactly where ever they ask me to sit. I have had a time, sometime last week, they changed my seat up to three times, and I obeyed. So I don't know when I insulted any usher. The only person I asked about salary is the lady who cleans the church and it is because I could not determine her salary from the records you gave me. Every single month of the whole year, the figures changed. From three thousand to ten thousand. She told me she was paid three thousand every month and that was all." She swallowed hard and took a deep breath.

"As for your assistant, Pastor John. He asked me what work I was doing for you. I told him you were in the best position to answer that question. He called me names including unbeliever and Jezebel and told me he would send me away from you; it was just a matter of time. He said I wanted to cause your ministry to fail and I would not succeed. I did not tell you because you already believed I was antagonising him. I took it as one of those terrible things you hear and throw away. Apart from that, I have had one or two sisters come to me that I should leave you alone, that you belong to them. I chose to discard all those words too because they mean nothing to me" she heaved. Her words racked his ears like an explosion of steam-whistles. He raised his head slowly to look at her. She stood up.

"I'll like to leave now" she said looking straight at the door.

"Please, Pam" he stood also and looked at her. "Sit down. Let's talk"

"If you have questions, you can ask, I am ready to leave so I'll remain standing"

"Pastor John…"

"Look, it's his word against mine and really, it's alright to believe him. I'm not trying to defend myself to you"

"I don't believe him. I believe you. Baby, I believe you" he made to touch her shoulder, but she hit his hand away.

"If you don't have anything to say again, please I'd like to go" she picked up her bag and started to walk to the door.

"Don't walk out on me" he said sternly. She stopped, standing rigidly. He sat back and stared at her back. He had been foolish to be so emotional about this. There was nothing he could say to stop her now. She was mad with him and she had every right to be. He assessed her rigid posture. He loved this girl, and he wasn't even sure she knew it. Or maybe she didn't know how much he loved her. Every time he tried to broach the subject of the proposal, she nailed it. Not even a maybe or a no?

"Love" he started quietly, "is like a miser in the dark his joys hide; it shakes like a windy reed your heart" he stood up and walked to stand behind her. "I feel intense love for you. It makes me excited and adventurous. But I also discovered that," he paused before placing his hand gingerly on one shoulder, "my love for you makes me defensive, instead of protective.

"Can you forgive me? I made a fool of myself today, believing him before you. I'd rather be your fool, Pam. Please hide me."

She turned to face him. His tears brought tears to her eyes. He pulled her into his arms and hugged her. But not for long.

There was a brisk knock on the front door and it opened. Pam reacted pushing back. Obasse acted more slowly and by the time the intruder came in fully, his hand was still holding on to hers. Pastor Jasper stopped short when he saw the two of them. Pam sniffed, embarrassed and faced the visitor with a tremulous smile.

"I was just leaving" she said. "We'll see tomorrow" she turned to Obasse. He nodded.

"Pastor Jasper, you're welcome" he said, "just give me a minute; let me see her off"

They left the house together and walked quietly to the road. He got her into a taxi and waved. They hadn't said a word to each other.

When he came back in, Pastor Jasper was sitting at the dining table, reading through a small Bible.

"My brother, I don't know o! What I just saw now simply nails the coffin" Jasper shook his head, closing the Bible in his hand with a snap.

Obasse slumped into the chair beside his friend and took a calming breath. He cleaned his face of imaginary sweat, and gazed into space. When he refused to say anything, Jasper continued talking.

"I didn't think I would meet her here" he said, trying to be civil. "You guys later decided to meet here?"

"Don't patronize me, Jasper" Obasse groaned. "You want to condemn me; do it"

"I didn't expect to see what I saw tonight. So are you ready to confess?"

"Oh please" Obasse stood up and walked to the window to peep out at nothing. His nerves were raw and much as he needed badly to talk to someone, he couldn't form the words.

"Did you ask her about John's allegations?"

"I did"

"And?"

"John lied to me" Obasse turned back to sit with his friend.

"Someone definitely lied but how are you sure it is Pastor John?" Jasper reasoned.

"Some of the things she said rhymed with John's. I believe her, Jasper. She has no reason to lie to me"

"And John has reason to lie to you?"

"You know what; she levied some allegations against John also"

"You see, you're now in the middle of the kind of controversy I was warning you against. What did she say John did to her? Raped her?" Jasper snickered.

"Called her names, and warned her to stay away from me" Obasse said, ignoring the derision.

"Good advice, if you ask me. Where did you get her from anyway?"

"She really is a nice person if you know her" Obasse sighed. "You don't even know her and you're so judgmental"

"She's not your type, Obasse. The best she can give you is her body. What kind of friendship are you keeping with a lady like that? She looks like someone straight out of a foreign magazine.

And I've never known you to keep such a close acquaintance with a female"

"What have you seen wrong with her?" he asked.

"She's loud, I mean pretty in a kind of loud way. She's too beautiful and obvious. Has she been a beauty queen before?" Jasper asked.

"Oh no" Obasse laughed for the first time at the description. "She said some ladies in church told her I belong to them. I wonder who would say such a thing like that"

"You refuse to tell me where you got her from? Did you visit a night club?" Jasper asked and Obasse burst into laughter. "She looks like that" he insisted. "That her hair is so long and wild. Is it natural? Does she always keep it flying like that? Or rather; maybe it's just hard to picture her with you."

"Who do you picture me with?"

"One of our church sisters. Lively, nice and very spiritual"

Obasse smiled and shook his head; then explained how he met Pam.

"I know Akim Duke very well. Oh so? But you do see what I mean if her sister is married to the likes of Akim Duke, a millionaire. People like her go for the highest bidder. Anyway, tell me what you have in common with Akim's wife's twin" Jasper said blandly.

"Her beauty. Her beauty draws out the man in me" Obasse said, looking at his friend's face. "I have never felt like this about a woman before. From the first time I saw her, there's been this very strong physical attraction"

"Physical attraction? That sounds so dangerous; she'll make you fall in the end. Beauty is vain o, my friend. Sincerely, she looks like a whore, a Jezebel. Women like that lie down for anyone who has the money. Girls like her will just be ticking men off their lives. She's ..."

"A virgin. She's a virgin"

"It's not true. She can't ..."

"I'm in love with her, Jasper. I proposed to her."

19

—·—

The same day Obasse sent the bound copy of his report to his headquarters, a chain of events began.

During the night after confronting Pam, he'd called her and they spoke for over two hours. He wanted to be sure she had forgiven him, and after convincing himself of that, tried to establish another bond, a stronger one. When he realized she was not going to talk about his proposal, still, he decided to move back to the safe and solid ground of friendship. Probably she would grow to love him.

He realized then that if indeed he was going to stick by her, it was better to make it clear to the people around him. And that night after hanging up, he composed a letter to his general overseer, through the head of finance. He copied the head of administration. He made no personal comments of his own in the letter, but only did an introduction to the report. He would send it by post first thing on Monday.

He stopped at Pam's office on Monday morning and fixed a date with her. He simply wanted to concentrate on knowing her better. And he wanted her to know him. They'd both attended their separate churches on Sunday and hung out in the evening for a drink. Jasper had been right. They were not in the same sphere. Her father had been a director-general before his death; his father was a police constable in the village. Her mother was the bursar at the federal university; his mother was a palm oil seller in the village, howbeit a prospering business. He was born and bred in the village, a self-made city man; she was a city girl from the start. And though he grew up an unbeliever; she was a church girl. But he did not see the differences. She was the woman who appealed to him. And though Jasper had categorically told him to forget it, he didn't know how that would happen. What he felt for her was stronger than anything he'd ever imagined possible.

"I have good news" she said excitedly as soon as he entered the office. "I now have a car" she shrieked.

"Really, huh. Tell me how it happened" he replied happily. He was so glad. That would settle her transportation woes.

"The university just gave Mummy a brand new official car so she's giving me her personal car" she smiled.

"I thought Mummy had an official car before" he asked.

"Mummy hated that old jalopy. She used her car more but they brought a brand new Peugeot to the house this morning to pick her. My car is parked outside. Come, let's go see it" she stood up and pulled him by the hand like a child. The white golf their mother had used was parked in the lot.

"Do you want to take me out for breakfast, madam?" he asked.

"I'll be delighted" she laughed. They got into the car and she drove to a fast food restaurant where they had a light breakfast, then she dropped him off at the church before going back to her office. He was very happy for her. Elle seemed to have taken a lead in life. Getting married first, and getting pregnant. And driving the car her husband gave her while Pam hopped commercial bikes. But Pam never behaved as though it was a bother to her. As wild and free as she looked, he'd discovered she was a very deep person. And she was very hard working. Despite all Akim's initial promises of upgrading and buying into their business, Pam had not pushed. And recently, Elle had forsaken the business altogether but Pam continued to work for both of them. She was considerate and kind; under that cold exterior was a real woman. Jasper and others would only have to learn to appreciate and know her better.

He packaged two copies of the report with his letter and went to the post office to send the parcel by registered post. It would be on the right table in a few days. In the mean time, he decided to alert John of what he had done so it would not be a sudden event to his assistant when the reactions came.

Pastor John was not a full time minister like Obasse. He worked as a teacher in a private secondary school and Obasse had to ask him to come to the office when he closed from work. He was counseling a man when John arrived. He rounded up his session with the member and asked John to come in and sit. He sat also with the file on his table.

"Pastor John, I did an audit of the church accounts for the last one year and sent it to the headquarters for General Overseer to see. I believe you know what that means"

"Okay. Is there anything I'm supposed to do?" John asked blandly.

"No. I already sent the report" Obasse repeated. "I just wanted you to know since you were the church administrator during that period. We may be required to comment on the report"

"So, why didn't you let me see it before you sent it, Pastor? If I have to comment on it, I should have known what you sent" he said. It was obvious he realized what it meant.

"This is your copy of the report" Obasse gave him the one on his table. John picked it up and browsed through. It was so obvious there was foul play in the records. Monthly salary changed every month. Honorarium expense stood out as a sore thumb. Things like pastor's expense, pastor's wife's expense and miscellaneous expense accounts were ridiculously high. John closed it with a snap and looked at Obasse.

"How can you send this kind of thing to the head office?" he demanded.

"Excuse me, Pastor?" Obasse blinked at the tone.

"Listen Pastor Obasse," he stood up angrily "if you think that this church is like the village church you're coming from then you're mistaken. If anything happens to me in this place, you will have only yourself to blame"

"Are you threatening me?" Obasse looked at him.

"It is not a threat. It is a vow. You will see yourself in this place" he flung the report in Obasse's face and stomped out, slamming the door behind him. Obasse sat, his mouth drooping, stupefied.

Later in the evening when he was alone with Pam, he recounted the ordeal.

"You should think of getting a job by the side, Obasse" she said softly. "What can I say? I'll feel responsible and guilty if you run into financial trouble because of this"

"I told you that's a no-go. You can't change my mind" he said. "He can't do anything to me." He said, reassuringly. She shrugged slender shoulders bared by the pink tiered halter neck top, over black combat trousers. She had driven home to change from her formal outfit before coming back to see him in the church.

"Well, he's a pastor, so I guess you're right..." she started. His phone rang and he picked it. He spoke for a few seconds and stood up.

"It's Jasper. I think he's waiting outside to see me. He's in a hurry. I'm sure John went to report to him" he stood up.

"I'll be going then" she stood up also.

"No, wait. He's in a hurry. I'll be right back." He stood up and left the office quickly.

When he got back, she was not in the office. He'd stood outside and not seen Jasper and angrily walked back to his office and she wasn't there. Her bag was there though so he assumed she'd gone to the bathroom to relieve herself. He sat down for a while and then stood up to check on her. That was when he heard the groan from the back of the altar. Before the sound of a dirty slap and cursing.

He rushed there. The altar of the church had been built with the intention of having a prayer room and some offices behind it, but the project was never quite accomplished and soon the back of the altar became like a free open space partially covered, that could be used as a meeting point. At night it was poorly lit and shielded both from the church and the outside world. A perfect place to do such an evil.

Pam was half-naked from the top to her waist, gagged, blind-folded and bound, struggling and weeping silently on the floor. John was crouching over in pain beside her, holding on to his groin and moaning. He had made the first initial sound in pain, probably after Pam must have kicked him. Obasse yanked his shirt off and covered her before thinking, and carried her hurriedly back to his office. He untied her quickly, leaving her halter neck top which had become rags around her waist.

Behind the altar of God!

He paced the small leg space in the office, trying to think as Pam fumbled to button his shirt up. They heard John's footsteps as he ran down the aisle and out of the church.

Obasse picked up Pam's bag and looked straight at her.

"Let's go" he said, stiffly. She stood to her feet, trembling. He took her by the elbow and half-dragged her out of the premises to her car. "Open the doors, I'll drive". She did as he bade, wondering why he was angry.

The tires screeched as he zoomed off into the night. It wasn't too late for dinner but he wasn't hungry. Nonetheless, he drove to a new restaurant on the outskirts of town and turned on her as soon as the car was parked.

"Why are you crying?" he snapped. "You asked for this didn't you?"

"How could you say that?" she sniffed, breathing hard and struggling to control her fury. "Your pastor almost raped me just now!"

"Has it crossed your mind why?" he asked. He barely moved his lips as he spoke.

"He's pervert. That's why, and I don't understand what is going on in your mind"

He pulled at the shredded pink top still hung around her waist and hissed. "This is why! You dress like a harlot. Why would men not want to tear you into pieces?" he cried.

She slapped him then. He didn't see it happen. She didn't see it happen either; because she looked at her hand and burst into tears. He clenched his fists, pooling all his energy to control the inane desire to retaliate, ignoring the sting on his cheek. He swallowed hard and closed his eyes.

"I didn't mean to do that" she whispered.

"But you did. I have never been slapped by a woman in my life"

"You annoyed me. How could you call me a harlot?" she moaned.

"Is it not true?" he opened his eyes and turned on her. "If you are not, why do you dress to seduce? Everyone is complaining about the way you look: your makeup, your hair, your dresses are short, your shoes are high!"

"Please take me home. You are annoying me!" she screamed.

"What happened tonight is not a mere coincidence"

"Yes, it is not. Your pastor just threatened you this morning" she said. He had not thought of that! But notwithstanding.

"He would have raped you, and then what would he gain? Will his raping you remove me as pastor?"

She opened the door and jumped out angrily, running into the night. He flew out of the car and ran after her, fearing he would not be able to curb his anger this time. He caught her just close to the main road and dragged her back to the car.

"Are you out of your mind?" he flung her against the chassis.

"Stop right there!" a male voice shouted behind them. He froze. Four men surrounded them in the dark parking lot, suddenly. The one who'd spoken held a gun to his head. "If you shout, you're dead" he snapped.

Obasse pulled Pam into his arms, using his body to shield her. One of the other men yanked her from his grip. She stifled a scream.

"You make noise and it's over" the first man said.

"Don't touch her. Take what you want" Obasse said slowly. The two men burst into laughter.

"Take what you want, boys" he repeated. One of the men started pulling at his trouser pockets. They removed his handset and slapped him hard when they didn't see any money. Pam stifled another cry, whimpering. Two of the men pushed her aside and started tearing at the shirt.

"No. No" she cried softly.

"If you touch her, fire will burn you" Obasse shouted in a whisper. "Fire will burn you." He began to sob, deep wracking sobs, calling on the fire of God. He did not know when the men left till Pam came to him where he was still leaning over the car, in the arresting manner.

"They've gone" she tapped him. "They've gone, let's go" she heaved. He turned sharply and caught her arms.

"Did they touch you? Did they hurt you?" he shook her gently. Sweat poured from his face though the night was cool, and he trembled more than she did.

"No. They said they didn't know you were a pastor; that they would never touch a pastor" she paused. "Or a pastor's wife" she looked at her hands.

"Oh thank you Jesus! Thank you Jesus" he slumped back against the side of the car and wept into his hands. She stood in front of him confused.

"Let's go" she mumbled.

"What would I have done if they had hurt you? How would I have forgiven myself? I was helpless. I couldn't do anything to help you!" he said, looking imploringly into her face.

"You helped with the weapon you had, the name of God. He saved us. Come let's go, please" she walked to her side of the door and opened it. He got into the car and drew a long breathe before turning to look at her.

"Are you sure you're alright?"

She nodded.

"Did John hurt you?" he asked. His head pounded, from the two slaps and the stress of the night. But he was more concerned for her. Fear for her safety had driven him to insane jealousy. Again, he had been irrational and temperamental. Two traits that was most unlike him. He put the car in gear, and began to drive back to town.

"He slapped me like ten times" she bit out.

"I'm so sorry. Tell me what happened" he requested pleadingly.

"As soon as you stepped out he came into the office. You know I had been sitting facing you, backing the door. He threw something over my head and gagged me. He slapped me like two or three times and suppressed me. He tied the blind fold and my hands and legs and carried me out. It all happened so fast. I suspected it was him because of his big body size but I didn't see him and he didn't say a word. I tried to struggle but his arms were like, Oh God, an iron vice or something... When we got to the back of the altar, he put me down and tore my blouse open and just started slapping me for like five minutes. I couldn't scream but I was crying and praying. Then he straightened and started unzipping himself. I couldn't see him but I felt he was still in front of me. I raised my two legs bound together with all my strength and tried to kick him back. I don't know how I hit his crotch... He screamed in pain; you came..."

"That was just God. I think we should report this. All of this" he said.

"No way." She protested.

"We have to. Jasper called me out of the office. He wasn't there when I got outside. I looked everywhere and because I didn't take my phone with me, I didn't call him back. I planned to do so when I got back in the office. When I didn't see you, I thought you'd gone to the toilet but when you still didn't come back, I felt uncomfortable. Just as I stepped out of the office, I heard his shout. He'll not get away with this, I promise you" he breathed.

"Just take me home, please" she sighed.

20

"The DPO in Federal Housing Police Station was my father's boss for a while in Obubra. He loves me very much and respects my father's integrity as a police man. Let's report this to him. Please" he said as they drove into Calabar town. She shrugged. They drove to the DPO's house in town first. Luckily the man was back at home. It wasn't too late to be out and about, at nine o'clock and he found no fault in their report. He escorted them back to the station where they made a detailed report of the incident at the out-of-town restaurant.

"We don't need to talk about John here" Pam whispered to Obasse. "I think that's in-house" she looked at him, piteously.

"We must. Please"

They wrote a detailed report of the church incident and the DPO then asked them to go home and rest.

"I would want to see Jasper tonight. I want to know where he was when he called me" he looked at her.

"No, I don't want to come with you. Your friend does not like me"

"That's not true. He ..."

"I want to go home" she insisted weakly.

He obliged her.

"I'll see you tomorrow. Please try and sleep" he looked at her as they both got out of the car at her house. He picked some change he saw in the car for his taxi fare

"Thank you, good night"

"I love you, Pam" he whispered. His hand brushed hers as he handed over the car keys and he pulled her to him. She resisted.

"It's late. I'm tired" she turned away and walked quickly into her house.

"Oh God please, don't let me lose her" he moaned and went to get a taxi to Jasper's house. He needed to get to the bottom of this.

Jasper was having a late dinner when Obasse entered his house. The appearance of his friend threw him aback. Obasse who was oblivious of the fact that he had given Pam his shirt earlier, was clad in a white cotton singlet, pulled out of his black trouser waist. His face was tear-streaked and strained.

"Jasper, good evening" he greeted before dropping into a seat. Jasper was slightly better-off than his friend. Though also unmarried, he was engaged to a lovely lady in his church. He also worked as a clearing agent at the port. His sitting room had a set of fairly-used real Italian leather set in brown and beige tones. A Persian rug in the same colour combination graced the terrazzo floor. His curtain was plain cream and beige with lace trimmings. The electronic shelf spotted every needed gadget; the 21" TV, a DVD player, a full surround stereo system and a complete CD rack.

He called on one of his two sisters, and a brother living with him, jumping up from his meal of semovita and soup, and washing him hand.

"Sidibe! Nsidibe!!" he shouted. A teenage girl ran in. "Bring drinking water and food" he commanded. Obasse's hand went up as he shook his head.

"No. I cannot eat" Obasse breathed. "I need to know, please…"

"Where are you coming from half naked?" Jasper gasped.

"It's a long story. We were attacked and I had to give my shirt to Pam"

"My God! Where is she now?"

"At home. I've taken her home" Obasse sighed. "I think I'll drink that water"

"Sidibe, bring water" Jasper called. "Who attacked you?"

"That's another long story. Please where were you when you called this evening?"

"Called who?"

"When you called me that I should come out of the church. You said you were in a hurry or something like that" Obasse took the water from Sidibe and the latter went back, leaving the two men in the parlour.

"I didn't call you tonight" Jasper said. He brought out his phone, and opened to dialled numbers. He scrolled down and up, shaking his head.

"You called me with your number" Obasse insisted, dipping his hand into his pocket for his phone before he remembered it had been taken. "Oh no!"

"I didn't call you o!" Jasper insisted. "What time did this call come in?"

"My phone was taken from me. I can't even check" he hissed. "But I know it was sometime before eight. Maybe seven, seven thirty."

"I've not even been with my phone since morning so how could I have called you? Tell me about this attack. Is it armed robbers?" Jasper asked concerned.

"Yes. They wanted to rape Pam. Oh God, they could have raped her!!" he heaved emotionally.

"Where were you people?"

Obasse recounted the ordeal briefly.

"God's name be praised. He honoured you" Jasper shouted. "Now this is what we are talking about. Yeah. We thank God o. What would you have told anybody?"

"I also want you to know this as a second witness. Pastor John also tried to rape her tonight" Obasse paused. "I know you don't really like her but she is a very decent person and I regret not defending her straight off last Saturday when you guys were castigating her."

"Which pastor John? I don't understand; he was with the armed robbers?"

Obasse explained everything to him in detail and Jasper sat numb for a few minutes.

"Now I see why you are in such a shaken disposition. That is terrible. What do you intend to do?"

"I will report it to the church board tomorrow. Thankfully they are meeting tomorrow" he sighed, drank his water and stood up. "I'll be leaving.

"Sit down" Jasper said. "I want to talk with you".

Obasse sat down slowly, looking at his friend.

"I don't understand all of what is happening here but your assistant pastor is not happy with you and that is not a good sign. He came to my office this morning and told me all the things you did with Pam. He's not happy at all and he has information that can destroy your life. Now you're saying he tried to rape Pam... it doesn't sound good at all. And he has witnesses, you don't" Jasper said softly.

"I don't understand" Obasse frowned. "What did I do with Pam?"

"Brother, you can be real with me. I love you like a blood brother and you don't need to hide your back from me" Jasper said.

"What are you talking about?" Obasse snapped.

"You've been having sex with Pam, he said he'd caught you there behind the altar several times and when you realised, you sent a report about the church accounts to headquarters, incriminating him" Jasper said. Obasse jumped up exclaiming. "Sit down, Obasse. I will believe you, whatever you tell me. We're friends, and covenant brothers"

"The closest I ever got to Pam was that hug you saw" Obasse whispered, dejectedly. He suddenly began to see a different picture that was coming to light. John had been brewing a negative publicity about his relationship with Pam and people had believed him. It would be his word against theirs. But then he had never told any of them he proposed to Pam. They just suddenly saw her face in the picture.

"I believe that, brother, sincerely. But John was in my house this evening. He came to pick me back to the church. He said he spied you two behind the altar but you had not seen him. He was panting and hysterical. He wanted us to catch you people red-handed. I begged him to go home and forget he saw anything. I don't think he did" Jasper replied, solemnly.

"I love that girl. Any attack on her personality will defeat me" Obasse heaved a heavy sigh.

"I don't see how you can get out of this, Obasse. You must have real hard facts to protect yourself and Pam."

Suddenly Obasse stood up. "You believe him too, don't you? He's convinced you" he accused.

"I will not lie to you, brother, yes I believed him. The odds are against you but you are my friend and my brother and I love you. I will help you any way I can but you are in trouble as it is!" Jasper snapped also getting to his feet.

"I have not done anything wrong!"

"I know. I believe you! But it does not look like that, does it?"

"You know" Obasse snorted, "Pam warned me. She said do the right thing, but be ready to suffer for it" he headed for the door.

"I pray she stands by you now" Jasper said, making Obasse stop short. "It's going to get real dirty. John is going for the jugular".

"No one else will" Obasse said emphatically and stomped out of the house.

21

—·—

It was dirtier than anyone imagined.

When Obasse reported to work the following morning, the board had conveyed an emergency meeting. They were waiting for him. He did not have much of a chance. He was shocked that every one of the twelve members of the board was in attendance. Pastor John was there with three ushers, Festus the office assistant, Mma Rose the cleaner and Ette Udoh the night security man. Obasse was immediately summoned before the board, and the allegations counted before him. They all surrounded his indecent and sinful relationship with Pam. When the chairman of the board finished with the tale of how John had ran to his house the previous night to tell him to come back to church to 'catch' pastor red handed, and how he had followed him and arrived just in time to see pastor and the said lady hurriedly driving away, with pastor in singlet alone. Some of the other board members gasped in shock. In truth, it had been Etteh Udoh who saw them leaving.

"Have you made up your minds about me on this matter?" Obasse asked harshly. It got the board very upset. Most of them didn't really know him well enough. He had only been their pastor for a couple of months. The few who knew him before were just dumbfounded by the whole tale.

"Pastor Obasse" the chairman of the church board spoke with controlled temper, "I will give you one more chance to defend yourself"

Suddenly Obasse felt like Jesus Christ, when the people asked him to cast the first stone on the adulterous woman. How dare they levy such allegations at him? He answered to no man. What would he say? It was true he was behind the altar with Pam last night. Though not alone. It was true he left the church premises hurriedly and in his underwear!

"My only defence is in God" he held his breath for a second. "He will judge me if my heart is true. I cannot defend myself to you. I'm sorry"

"Does anyone have anything to say? This is a very crucial meeting and that is the only reason why we will leave our tight schedules to come here at this time of the day, and I believe we are all anxious to get back to our offices and businesses" the chairman said, looking round the group. No one said a word. "Well, since no one has said anything, and Pastor Obasse has nothing to say to us in his own defence, I will say he proceeds to step aside from his duties as the pastor of this church, without pay, till such a time as we finalise our investigations and decide on the appropriate form of discipline for the pastor" he concluded. "Thank you very much".

The meeting adjourned. The board members stood up and left, murmuring amongst themselves. Ette Udoh hung around the pews; Mma Rose fidgeted at the end of one row; Festus leaned against the wall. Pastor John spoke briefly with the ushers before they left. Obasse sat in a meditative mode, his feet wide apart, his two hands loosely clasped against his lower lip, his eyes half-closed.

"Remove your personal effects from the office" John stood in front of him and said. He looked at him blankly and nodded. Who cared? John could play the hero now, he wasn't bothered. Truth will out, they say and he believed it. And he sat there in the main hall of the church till John finally left, and Festus went about his business and Ette Udoh left and Mma Rose went back to her work. He stood up and went to his office. His 'personal effects' were not that many. He picked his copy of the report from his drawer and a Bible. He looked round the stuffed office for any other thing. Nothing. If he came back, he would clean this place out. The store and library will go behind the altar. In fact, the back of the altar will cease to be legendary.

"Pastor" Festus called, clearing his throat. Obasse had not heard him come in and he looked up from where he had been staring blankly into space. Festus, a slight framed man was probably in his mid-thirties, though he could be younger or much older. When Obasse took over as the pastor, he'd interacted with all the church staff pleasantly, encouraging them to work with him. He took an immediate liking to Festus, who though was most likely older than he was, took his job seriously. Though a married man with three children, none of his family issues had come before his work. And Obasse knew that was integrity because the paltry five thousand naira being paid by the church could barely feed a child for a month. He had been waiting for reaction to the report before he did his own modifications to the church reward system.

"Hmm?"

"I don't know what is happening here..." he stammered. "Et-teh said..."

"Festus, don't bother yourself about anything" Obasse stood up, grabbing his effects. He pulled on his tie to loosen it. "Just remain true to yourself and to God" he walked past the other man, who stood gaping at him.

"Pastor, I know something is wrong but..."

"Festus, go back to your work" Obasse rebuked softly. He walked into the main church hall and saw John discussing with one of the members of the church. Obasse nodded briskly as he walked past. He could only imagine what the expression on the man's face meant.

He went straight to Pam's office and found it locked, to his utter dismay. That sounded like very bad news. She never joked with her job and whatever would keep her away couldn't be nice. Even whenever she had to lock the office to go out, she always left a word with Alice or other neighbours. No one had seen her or Elle. He headed for her house.

The first thing he noticed was Elle's car, parked outside. He hoped he would find an advocate in her if need be. His feelings were jumbled and mixed and he wasn't even sure how Pam would handle the recent development.

He knocked once sind opened the door. There was no one in the parlour so he called out. The house lady, Beatrice, came out of the kitchen towel-drying her hands.

"Good morning" Obasse greeted.

"Good morning sir. May I help you?"

"I'm asking for Pam" he said.

"Please take a seat" she said, and left. "Your name, please?"

"Obasse"

Elle came out a few minutes later. Her pregnancy still did not show but she had added a few ounces. Obasse stood up to receive her.

"Hah, Pastor Obasse, good morning" she greeted nicely. "How are you?"

Obasse was not deceived by the sweetness; Elle was a naturally cool as cucumber lady. You could never quite determine if the heat was on in her life or not. Unlike her sister. If all was well Pam would have come out except if...

"I'm fine, Elle. How's Pam?" he asked anxiously.

"She doesn't want to see anybody" not one to mince words like her twin, Elle shook her head and sat down.

"She doesn't want to see me"

Elle shook her head. Obasse sat down slowly. What would he do now? He saw this coming after last night.

"She told you everything" it was a statement of fact.

"And Mummy, and Akim" Elle sighed. "She was hysterical last night after you dropped her off. Mummy called Akim and I and we came over to the house. This morning Mummy spoke with the DPO to drop all the charges and disregard the reports. It was Pam's decision"

Obasse held his head in his hands, unable to react. What a mess!

"Mummy is not very happy with you right now. She just left for her office this morning; thank God you didn't meet her." Elle said. "She blames you for everything, and for dropping Pam off just like that last night. In that condition" Elle sighed. "I didn't even know anything was going on between the two of you. I'm sorry" she said softly. So like Elle.

"I'm sorry. I feel so bad. After I proposed to her, I thought she would..."

"You've proposed to her? You guys are engaged?" Elle gasped.

"She didn't tell you?" Obasse counter-asked, just as shocked. He thought sisters told themselves everything all the time.

"No. She did not!"

"We're not engaged though. She refused to give me a reply. Not yes, not no, not even wait or maybe. She just refused to reply. I just thought maybe she needed to get to know me better and all" Obasse's voice droned. It was no use now. Pam had shut him out. Not telling anybody about the proposal was a colossal failure on his part to win her heart. Not even her sister!

He jumped to his feet, suddenly. There was nothing much to say. He had come to her for comfort and to offer his. But there was none to be had. Her request to have the cases reported closed permanently meant she really didn't want to see him again. Well, this was his hour of need. Of course she didn't know yet the heat was on in the church, but would telling make a difference? He was afraid to find out.

"I must go now" he said. "Thank you for everything" he walked out of the house without waiting for a response.

Long after he had gone, Elle remained seated in the parlour till Pam walked out slowly to meet her. Her eyes were red and puffy from crying through the night and getting little or no sleep at all.

"He's gone" she whispered as though to convince herself. She clutched her cotton housecoat to herself as a suckling child would his mother.

Elle looked up at her with mixed feelings.

"He said he asked you to marry him!" It was a direct accusation.

22

The gloom of the day deepened when Obasse got home to find his mother. She had come in a little earlier. He was in the least mood to attend to visitors but had to sit quietly and listen to more tales of woe from home. His father was terribly sick and they needed money. He had none. His salary was not due for another week and he doubted the board would approve it under the current situation. But as all mothers were, she noticed he was troubled.

"Your sister said she will come and visit, because I called her first" she added, trying to lighten the matter. "She even sent some money. She paid into your brother's account. I've sent him to go and withdraw it" she said. He nodded. "I brought palm oil for that nice lady who cooked for you last time. And some to sell too" she paused. "To raise money." He nodded. "I want to eat and rest, then we can talk about what is bothering you."

He nodded.

Jasper came in later in the evening to visit. Earlier Obasse had sent Okey to Pam's house with the palm oil his mother brought for her. He wished he could go himself but could not bring himself to face another rejection. By the time Jasper came in the evening, he had had a long talk with his mother and decided to resign himself to his fate, taking one day at a time. He sat mute as Jasper gave him the update of his situation.

"Pastor John was at my place" he'd started before going into full detail of the whole ordeal, which Obasse had passed through. "Have you told Pam about all this?"

"Jasper, what do you want?" Obasse snapped, losing his temper. Had his friend come to taunt him? "You want to know if you were right about her, if I was wrong. What do you want?"

Taken aback, Jasper frowned. "I want nothing more than to help, sincerely. Look at you. If anyone persecutes you, they persecute me" Jasper said softly.

"I don't want any help right now, Jasper. Honestly. The only way you can help me is by going away from me. Go back to John and get any information you wish"

"You know, I was thinking about that call you talked about, yesterday" Jasper stated. Obasse hissed. "I was in my office when John came in that morning. I took a call from that phone. He sat with me in my office lamenting over and over again. He spent over an hour before I stood up and went outside, just to discourage him and send him on his way. Immediately I came back, he stood up to go. I thought my ploy had worked"

Obasse shrugged.

"But I never saw that phone again until after John had left my house in the night!" Jasper said, ruminating. "I didn't even need it until a brother came in the afternoon and asked why I didn't pick my phone. I looked for it everywhere! I called the number over hundred times throughout the day, no one picked it. After John left my house that night, my phone began to ring.

I shouted ha, my phone and laughed at myself for forgetting it at home. It was under the couch. John was calling to tell me he had reached home safely. All the missed calls were reflected in my phone but that single call to you was no where to be found" his tale was compelling, but Obasse did not pay attention. "I saw my phone before I saw John yesterday, and I didn't see it again until after I'd seen John again. After the call and the rape attempts"

"Look, that is very fine investigative reasoning, Jasper, but I'm not interested" Obasse said. "I have no intention of defending myself to you or any body else. I have my team, they know the truth and they believe me."

"Obasse please. I've known you since our school days, I believe you. It's only just that this kind of thing has happened before, and you confessed then..."

"How can you refer to that? I was a young convert. I told you I had lusted after Bessy and slept with her, and that was all! I never told you I loved her or proposed to her!! How can you compare me at that time to now?" Obasse yelled.

"The last time I saw you with a woman; it was Bessy." Jasper said calmly. "It's only normal to put two and two together. If I have queried you it is only to brainstorm with you"

"I understand, thank you. But that's all for me. I want to pull through this on my own; in my own way. I don't need your help, thank you" Obasse stood up and walked into his room, leaving Jasper in the parlour. It was the second time he would uncharacteristically walk out on his friend.

Jasper was so shocked he went to find Pam.

After a series of calls; to someone who had Akim's number; then to Akim to get the house address, Jasper visited Pam.

She refused to see him also.

Two days later, Elle came to Obasse's house. She met only his mother. The older woman was planning on going back to the village since she had received the monies her daughter, Idik, sent from Abuja. Obasse had spoken to some of his old parishioners about the palm oil she brought, and she had successfully sold all at a higher price than she bargained. Though she didn't have all the money she needed, she decided to return and care for her husband who she had left in the care of her last daughter, Kwam, who was at home on a short break from school. Doctors had diagnosed Ovat with typhoid fever.

"Good afternoon ma. My name is Elle Duke" Elle greeted, bending slightly as was the custom when greeting an older person.

"My daughter, welcome. Please sit down" Nancy answered pleasantly.

"Thank you, ma. Please is pastor at home?"

"No. He went out. I don't know when he will be back" she replied.

"Wow" Elle sighed. "Huh, you're his mother" she asked.

"Yes."

"Ok. I actually came to thank you for the palm oil you sent to my sister"

"Oh. Ok. Your sister took care of him that time?" Nancy lit up. Okey had only told them he didn't meet the lady and only left the palm oil. "Heh, thank you o. Ha, he was very sick and he told me how you and your sister came and cooked for him and took care of him" she said happily. "Thank you"

"It's nothing. He's our pastor and we have to take care of him. So we're very glad. The palm oil is very sweet o, Mama. Thank you. In fact, our Mummy also sent greetings to you" Elle said sweetly.

"Hey, it's nothing. It's the little I can do" Nancy said.

Elle stood up. "Ma, please greet pastor for me. I have to go now."

"Ok my dear. Thank you" Nancy also stood up.

"Huh, I don't know when you'll be going back home but I just wanted on my own to give you a token for your transport because I may not see you or Pastor before you return" Elle pushed a slim envelope into Nancy's hand. The older woman rejected it immediately.

"No o. Ha, for what? Thank you o, ha. My son has very nice people around him o, thank God" Nancy exclaimed, resisting yet accepting the gift.

"It's nothing ma. I have to leave" she headed for the door. Nancy followed her. Elle noticed she was a very smart woman, for her fifty-something or sixty-something age, which was hard to determine. She saw Elle to her car outside, despite the protests from the younger woman.

When Nancy opened the envelope Elle had pushed into her hand, she found ten clean bills of one thousand naira notes. Ten thousand naira!

"Hey!" she screamed. It was more than she needed to go back home.

23

—·—

The days flew by monotonous and colorless. Obasse buried himself in an aptly improvised routine. He woke up early as always and went out to a nearby church where he spent the whole day. He hardly ate more than a light meal at the end of the day. Though he told himself, it was not a time to take a long fast; it was indeed a time of deep reflections. He remembered the judgment that had been dispensed with formality on him. The frosty calm Pam had sat with eyeing him on that last evening with her, receiving his warmth, yet refusing it as he would now come to realize. Like a dream she had vanished from his life, taking the same swift exit as her entry had been. Most of the day, he just sat in the pews thinking about her. But he prayed also, and he studied. And a lot of the time, he meditated on the goodness of God. God had brought Pam to him. He had given him opportunities to affect her life and the lives of several others. Most importantly he reminisced; God had tested his endurance. When he was dating Bessy, he had taken liberties; undue liberties with her. Though he had not become a pastor then, he was a believer and she was a believer. As soon as he started having sex with her, he knew he would never marry her and though he had finally confessed to his closest ally, Jasper, the church had never heard about it. Bessy had been a student at the time while he worked. When she finished her studies, she left town. For good. He had retraced his steps and reconciled with God.

But he had secretly feared the next time he would be attracted to a woman. Would he not fall again? Several times, he had been tempted to take a woman but he had fought the urge like a demon. It was one of the reasons he had hoped to marry quickly, avoiding the temptations of a long courtship. But then, his spiritual father had always admonished him to take care of himself first. "Build up yourself on your most holy faith... be selfish... think about yourself; your salvation; your needs; your desires; your vision; your purpose; your future. Think about the consequences of sin!" Those were the things he'd done with Pam. He'd loved her from his own selfish vintage. His feelings for her were at his own terms and from there he'd been able to curb irrepressible passions. And he had not been half as attracted to Bessy as he was to Pam. She was for keeps. How it would happen he did not know. Neither did he care.

He prayed for her also. And he prayed concerning his own predicament. He hadn't heard anything from the church board but he attended services regularly. The same evening service on the day he was asked to step aside, the church had been informed and John had been asked to take over as the pastor in charge. Obasse had sat quietly at the back of the hall, groaning with disdain, and battling bitterness like a man fighting for his life.

After that day, he had withdrawn into quiet solitude. Nothing anyone said moved him. Some members had approached him, seeking to gossip under the guise of genuine concern. He had withstood them. Resolved, he attended every church service, and suffered John's disjointed coded messages. It was patience with an expiry date, he encouraged himself. Meanwhile, he focused on himself. The DPO reported the request Pam had made through her mother and him, and he concurred but the law man refuted the request. As long as a crime had been committed, and reported, it was no longer the responsibility of the complainant. DPO informed Obasse he would invite John for questioning.

"I will not be involved sir, if the lady is not" he'd pleaded. He assumed his plea had been accepted since he did not get any further information from the DPO. On the other hand, he did not also get any feedback on the finance report that triggered the following events. He assumed here also that John had been summoned and lied his way out of the ordeal.

The expiry date of his anxious patience approached sooner than he expected. It happened two weeks later.

A day to this, he got home as usual from the nearby church, humming. He opened the front door and stood stock still at the sight he beheld. Pam sat cross-legged at the dining area sipping juice from a glass cup. She was talking rapidly with Atai.

Atai.

He had seen her car parked outside but it hadn't registered to him she was the one. The two looked towards him as he stepped in and Atai smiled. "Pastor, welcome" she greeted jovially.

He did not respond. He gazed at Pam, his gaze full of unconquerable hopefulness. She tried to hide a faint quivering smile but failed woefully. She wore the yellow dress she had worn the day he hugged her. Her hair was piled high on her head in a neat pack, the curls dangling about her face. He'd never seen her style the hair like that? It left him dumbfounded. His soul compressed into a single agony of prayer. *Lord, Lord, Lord.*

"Pastor, come in. We were waiting for you" Atai giggled shyly, drawing his attention to her.

"What are you doing here?" he croaked.

"Come in" Pam said. "There's something I want to tell you".

His mouth quivered with pleasure. "The angels of God have come down" his speech faltered. Constraint became excruciating as he moved to stand beside her. What a wonder, he marveled.

"How are you?" she spoke with sweet severity that turned his brain inward out. He strangled a fierce tide of desire that welled up within him. "I planned to surprise you" she gently took his hand in hers.

"You have" he whispered.

She recaptured herself with difficulty at the tone of his voice and continued. "It's a long story but I want to tell you in detail. Atai will help me" she spoke with unhurried eagerness. "Won't you sit down?"

It was a night of stupefying surprises, but one he was ready to wait out. He drew the seat next to hers and sat down, her warm hands sandwiched one of his.

"After you left me that night, I became hysterical when Mummy asked me where I was coming from. She couldn't handle it and called in Elle and Akim. They succeeded in calming me. But they thought it was as a result of fright of the ordeal. In actual fact, I was scared to death that I could have lost you" she swallowed and smiled at him shyly. He blinked. "Yes, Obasse. I love you and I want to be your wife"

"No!" he burst into a laughter that graduated to a guffaw. "Yes!"

"Yes. But that's not why I came tonight. Atai and I and Elle and Akim have been working since that day. When Elle accused me of stalling your proposal, I realized I had a role to play and much as I was scared of being a pastor's wife, it seemed to be my portion". He pulled her up from her seat and drew her into a tight hug. Atai shouted so they'd see she was there and behave themselves.

"Go back to wherever they got you from" he mumbled laughingly.

"Pam, tell him" Atai said.

"He won't let me breathe" she giggled. He stepped back immediately and she made a face.

"You con" he laughed.

"Come and sit down, honey. Here's the big one." She pulled him back to the seat. Her words were like a balm to his weary soul. He allowed himself to be dragged back into his seat. "Tomorrow, you're going to face the board again" Pam said.

A dark shadow crossed his face, hanging the lingering smile about his lips.

"I think Pam is too excited to tell you, Pastor" Atai interrupted. "You see, after Elle spoke with Pam, she decided to come and give you her reply. But your brother came with the palm oil gift from your mother, and hinted about the trouble at the church. He, of course, was in church when it was announced. So Pam and Elle went back to the DPO that the case should not be dropped. The DPO said he'd told you it was now a state case and he would do his own job. He took Pastor John for questioning and detained him for a night. He was released on bail the following day because of lack of evidence."

"We did not want to involve you because John had been released by the police but we needed someone in the church, who would blend easily, and who liked you a lot" Pam stated.

"And someone mischievous enough to have done what I did in your office" Atai added. "Please forgive me, though".

"I remembered what you said about Atai's mother and we went to look for her. When we finished with our request, she agreed…"

"For no other reason than just to feel belonging to someone or something" Atai said.

"But we fell in love with her. She's a very adorable person" Pam smiled. "Atai helped us to know what was going on in the church. She made herself close to John and his wife to get information. They saw her as a new and needy member and allowed her to get close to them"

"To what purpose?" "Obasse asked, unimpressed.

"I wanted to know the outcome of the report you sent to the headquarters" Pam said. Obasse shook his head.

"By snooping?" he asked.

"I needed to know somthing, Obasse. And remember I have my own personal grudge against John."

"Pastor Jasper we discovered was also very close to Pastor John. I was very suspicious of him because I always knew him to be your best friend" Atai said.

"He changed camps." Obasse snorted.

"'Twas what we thought. We were snooping around the office late one night when he opened the door. Elle and Atai and I froze, thinking, 'shit'. We looked like rabbits caught in the light. He burst into laughter and asked us what we were doing there. Jasper is now our strongest ally. We'd gone to the office to search; he came to pick up. GO had sent a letter acknowledging receipt of the report and stating investigators would come in. The letter stated the date and time and people coming. We ran to my office and duplicated the letter and returned it. When they came, John feigned ignorance. He said he didn't receive any letter and that you were on a standby. They checked the records of the church and found a totally different state of things, and left with their report" Pam said at length.

"I still don't get your motive or what you hope to achieve"

"We now have a lot of facts; all the documents you used to prepare your report are lost but we have duplicates. We were just waiting for the board to summon you back and we know what they want to do with you. Then we do what we want" Atai said.

"I see" Obasse mumbled.

"We have a long list of accomplices; including Mma Rose and Etteh Udoh" Pam said.

"Interesting" Obasse softened his frown to a loose smile. "I guess Festus is also on board?"

"John sacked Festus immediately you left. He confronted him about you and John fired him".

"I never noticed. Now that you say it, I wasn't seeing him in church which was unusual".

"So darling, you'll get a message tonight or in the morning, they'll summon you for a meeting tomorrow. John put a lot of pressure on them to fire you. They'll probably do that tomorrow, we don't know" Pam said. "I want to be there with you".

"No, Pam dear. You don't know how bad that can be" he protested.

"I want to be with you from now on, through anything you may pass through… except of course…" she stood up and moved away from him. "If you have changed your mind about your proposal to me?"

"Of course not. You know I can never stop loving you. I don't want you to pass through any stress. They may insult you…" he stood up and stood behind her.

"I want to be by your side. I wasn't there when you faced them the first time and I'm still trying to forgive myself for that" she turned into his arms.

"My love" he whispered.

24

— · —

They walked into the church hall, holding hands.

Pam wore a lemon skirt suit with a dress scarf in green and maroon tones. She wore high maroon sandals. Obasse wore a black suit with a stiff white shirt and lemon and grey striped tie. They made a striking couple. Their presence threw the panel off balance; jealousies and animosities pricked their sluggish blood to tingling. Obasse walked round shaking and greeting the board members confidently with his right hand, while the left remained interwoven with Pam's right. She followed suit grudgingly. They had not agreed to be cordial but the effect was stunning. The members looked at themselves as Obasse smiled and joked and asked after their families and businesses. They had seen him last only two days ago and he had been his withdrawn self. They concluded he was stage-acting.

They sat down and made eye contact with each of the twelve members; and Pastor John who they already knew would be there but thought he had appeared as a surprise.

"Pastor Obasse Edim, you're welcome" the chairman of the board greeted dourly. His snubbing of Pam obvious. She stilled and trampled on the inward protest; Obasse squeezed her hand in support. "I am surprised you came here with... her" he waved at her with disdain. "I think she should leave" he continued. She stood or rather *sat* her ground with the most perfect dignity. After a pause of complete silence, Obasse cleared his throat.

"We're waiting for you to continue, sir" he said softly, his steely tone sliced through the silence as surely as a butcher's knife.

"After all the investigations concerning the allegations levied against you, we will like to ask you some questions, before we take a decision" the chairman said briskly.

"Okay, sir" Obasse said respectfully. The chairman nodded towards the secretary, a middle aged woman who Obasse had known for a while in the church circles. She looked into a sheet of paper in her hand.

"Pastor Obasse, did you sleep with a lady called Bessy during your days as a worker in the church?" she asked blandly. Her question threw Obasse off guard, and it was Pam's gentle squeeze of his hand that kept him from blurting out an insult. She had told him to be calm and whatever they said could be discussed later after their verdict.

"Don't lose your temper. If you do, they win" she had admonished. It had been a surprise to her as well because she had always been the hot-tempered one.

"I and Bessy did have sex together over a period of fifteen months. Quite regularly too" he responded simply.

"By regularly, you mean everyday?" someone asked him.

He gave a short laugh and shook his head. "Perhaps once or twice a week on the average" he said.

"You feel no remorse for that sin?" someone barked at him.

"I did feel remorse. I asked God for forgiveness and repented of the sin. It never repeated itself. I became serious with my relationship with God" he said. The chairman snickered.

"You did not openly confess to the church?"

"No I did not"

The chairman wrote something down.

"Did you sleep with a lady called Pamella?" the secretary asked.

"I don't know any lady called Pamella" Obasse replied.

"What is the name of the lady sitting beside you?" Pastor John asked, fuming.

"Pamelle".

A hiss went round the room.

"Did you sleep with Pamelle?"

"No. I cannot sleep with my helpmeet before marriage". The comment was ignored.

"What were you doing behind the altar on the said night? You know the night we refer to so don't be funny!"

"I went to rescue my Pam from being raped by Pastor John" he said.

Pastor John jumped to his feet in anger.

"What insolence. You had better respect yourself, Obasse! Is that why you were half-naked when Elder and I came to the church to catch you?" John said.

"Why were you half-naked?" the secretary asked.

"Pastor John had torn her blouse. I had to cover her with my shirt"

"Sir, this is not true" John said, shaking with indignation.

"How many times did you have sex with Pamelle since you met her?"

"Nil"

"When was the last time you had sex with Pamelle?" the secretary read from her note.

"It hasn't happened yet."

Pam squeezed the cool hand clamped in hers with every question.

"When was the first time you had sex with this lady called Pamelle?"

"A time and date does not exist"

"Why would you choose the back of the altar of the house of God to fornicate with Pamelle?"

"I would not dare"

"Then where was the first place you used for sex with Pamelle?"

"A venue does not exist"

"Where do you normally use to have sex with Pamelle?"

"A venue does not exist"

"Why would you, a man of God, defy the authority of God and openly fornicate with Pamelle?" the secretary looked up.

Pam gave Obasse's hand a hard squeeze as he twitched with restrain.

"It has never happened" he spoke with a uniformity of emphasis that made his words stand out like the raised type for the blind.

The secretary looked at the chairman and nodded. "That is all I have for him, sir" she said, closing her book.

"Thank you, Madam" the chairman cleared his throat. "We have heard from Pastor Obasse, and by all standards from his responses, he is not guilty. However, we can not take his word alone in all fairness to all parties concerned, we have to match his responses with the investigations we carried out." The elder paused. "Pastor John, you ran to my house and asked me to come and see Pastor with a woman at the back of the altar, and I followed you. When we got here, we only saw Etteh Udoh, who said they left in a hurry, pastor wore only singlet and trousers, Pamelle wore a man's shirt" he flipped to the next page of a typed report he read from. "With the help of Pastor John, I met Pastor Jasper who has been of tremendous help to Pastor John. Pastor Jasper then introduced me to the DPO of Federal Housing Estate Police Station who acknowledged that Pastor Obasse reported the case of attempted rape at the church on the same night. Pastor Jasper said he came to his house also that night to cross-check a false call from him, which had taken him away from Pamelle for the period of time she was abducted from his office.

In addition, I personally interviewed the church staff. And above all, a delegate who came in from the headquarters to investigate a record fraud of the church accounts. After putting all the pieces together and presenting documents which Pastor Jasper gave copies of to me, and matching them with the documents Pastor John gave to the investigators, all parties concluded in favour of Pastor Obasse" he looked at Obasse and nodded. It was then Obasse realised he had been pressing Pam's hand so hand. He relaxed the hand.

"I am so sad to say that Pastor John fooled all of us. He is the culprit here. And I invited him to state this. Pastor Obasse and Miss Pamelle, please accept our apology…"

"This is all rubbish" Pastor John stood up angrily and matched out of the church premises.

"I have given a copy of this report to the DPO and sent one to the headquarters. Pastor Obasse is hereby fully reinstated as the parish pastor of this assembly, and all his outstanding salary and allowances will be paid today unfailingly. We are sorry for jumping to conclusions based on what Pastor John told us. We have now seen his plot to cover up his misdeeds with the former pastor by setting you up. We also want to assure you that the law enforcers are taking over the case from here. We congratulate you and Miss Pamelle," he looked round the panel. "Does anyone have anything to add or subtract?"

"You have spoken all our minds, Elder" the secretary said. "Thank you sir for your time and for getting to the bottom of this scam".

"Pastor Obasse, would you want to say anything?"

"I want to formally announce my engagement to Miss Pamelle Ukpabi. I will announce our wedding date when it has been fixed. Thank you very much also for your fairness and objectivity. I hold no grudges, neither does my fiancée" he said softly, looking round at each of them.

"Well, we can call for an adjournment" the chairman said. The men and women all stood up and shook hands with both of them before leaving.

They remained seated there, alone in the church hall, holding hands as tightly as they had when they came in.

"He planned to rape me, alert you I was there, then catch both of us there so he'd weave his story around that" she said.

"God made him foolish to plan such a thing. Just to blow it up in his face" he said.

"Jasper really did it for us"

"Yeah. He's a great man"

"Sorry about the two weeks of suspension."

"It was the best two weeks I had in recent times. I became the bride of Jesus."

"Better than the weeks we had together before the two weeks."

"Don't tempt me."

He chuckled. She laughed.

THE END

ARE YOU SAVED?

All that is written in this book may not be of much use to you if you haven't yet given your life to Christ. We cannot take difficult decisions unless we have the Righteous and Wise One that is greater than the devil to help and choose for us. The Bible says that greater is He that is in us, than He that is in the world I John 4:4. And we wrestle not against flesh and blood but against principalities, against powers, against the rulers of the darkness of this world, against spiritual wickedness in high places Ephesians 6:12.

This is why I want to encourage you to take this important decision if you haven't yet given your life to Christ. I took this decision twenty years ago and I haven't regretted it even for one day. Please pray this prayer of faith if you are willing to surrender your life to God:

Lord Jesus, I honour you. I praise you and I acknowledge you that you are Lord. I know I am a sinner and I ask that you forgive me all my sins. I want you to be my Lord and personal Saviour. Wash me clean and give me grace to serve you wholly from now on. Come into my heart to reign supreme. In Jesus' name I pray. Amen.

Praise God, you are born again.

Now that you have prayed this prayer of faith, I admonish you to:

1 Get a Bible, and read it everyday (Start from the first four books of the New testament to familiarize yourself more with your new Commander-in-Chief, Jesus Christ)

2 Pray everyday.

3 Attend a Living Church

4 Introduce yourself to the Pastor and seek further teaching (you can join the foundation class and activity group in church – you are hence making yourself available to work for God)

5 Tell others about your salvation.

May God help you in Jesus' name. Amen.

THE NIGERIAN CHILD – MY VISION

Hab. 2:2 Then the LORD answered me and said: "Write the vision And make it plain on tablets, That he may run who reads it.

More than before, it's time for the well-to-do to cater for the less-privileged. Over the past few years, the Lord has laid this burden for THE NIGERIAN CHILD on my heart and I believe it's time to spread the vision. I have a desire to help and to instigate help for THE NIGERIAN CHILD. There are currently five areas of help I have been able to identify.

1.   THE MARKET-SCHOOL PROJECT: this vision is aimed at eradicating street and market hawking in the long run. The strategy is to erect schools in market places where children hawking can take a few hours out to learn and then go back to their jobs. It is a long term project and a highly capital intensive one.

2.   THE BREAD AND MILK PROJECT: bread and milk will be given in the morning time to children trekking to school

just before school resumes. It can be done once a month, once a week or everyday. Or as rampantly as the provision is available. It is not very capital intensive and as little as ₦50 or $0.35 (US dollar) can feed a child with bread and warm milk

3.   THE UMBRELLA PROJECT: to help alleviate the suffering of children who hawk on the streets (while we work towards eradicating hawking on our streets), by providing umbrellas especially during the rainy season. The umbrellas can also be useful during the scotching hot weathers. Umbrellas of different sizes will be given depending on the size of the child. Prices of umbrellas range from ₦350.00 to ₦500.00 or $2.50 to $3.50 (US dollar).

4.   THE SORT-A-CHILD PROJECT: which is aimed at helping at least a child in whatever capacity you can. It can be by paying a sick child's hospital bills, buying food and clothing for a child or paying a child's school fees. It can be as long as a life-time commitment or a one-time affair.

5.   THE STUDENT CARE PROJECT: for secondary and tertiary students who can't afford their school fees. The idea is to help through the bob-a-job initiative.

THE NIGERIAN CHILD vision is not another non-governmental, money-spinning organisation. It is service to God and provision for THE NIGERIAN CHILD. It can be done privately or corporately. The important thing is to help a NIGERIAN CHILD.

I beg to challenge EVERY CHURCH IN NIGERIA to adopt the SORT-A-CHILD PROJECT or as the Lord lay it on our hearts.

HELP!
Signed - *THE NIGERIAN CHILD*

One

The bell tolled and the girls hurried towards the exit of their dormitories. It was time for manual labour. Anna clenched the rosary in her hand tighter as she ended her soft prayer. She had not been able to let go of the beads she claimed helped to discipline her to pray, despite the fact that she had given her life to Christ, become born again, and joined the charismatic catholic movement. She tucked the rosary into her house-wear pocket and turned as Banke rushed in to the corner to hurry her up.

"That's the second time" Banke snapped as she rushed away. Anna slipped into her slip-ons and rushed out, jamming the door behind her. She and Banke, her best friend, joined the throng of students going to the dining hall from where they would be distributed to their various points of duty. It was 4p.m. on the first Thursday of the month, when the labour prefect took charge. On other Thursdays, manual labour was from 4 to 6p.m but each house prefect took charge.

The bell rang three times. The first was to call the students. The second to warn the students. The last was to punish the students and woe-betide a student who got caught in the third; especially on a labour day. While all Thursdays were dedicated to labour, the first was conducted generally. All others were done locally in the dormitories. Banke and Anna fell in line just as the third bell went.

"God save you" Anna muttered and giggled breathlessly.

The labour prefects were four in number and each assigned to the four houses, Blue, Green, Red and Yellow. Student house-wears were according to the colour of their houses. The girls wore checker dresses while the boys wore the check short-sleeved shirt and khaki shorts. Most of the senior boys, especially the final year students wore theirs as Bermuda shorts or knickerbockers. The school indulged them. Every month, the head prefect rotated the labour prefects and today, to Anna's chagrin, Ojaks was in charge of her house, Red house. Ojaks was actually named Bode Subomi. For whatever reason, everyone called him Ojaks. He was a mean senior boy who apportioned boys and girls alike. Every month, students prayed Ojaks would go to another house and not theirs. He was a six-footer male with developed muscles like a real adult. Rumours had it that he was over twenty years old, but no one was to know.

Ojaks stood rigidly in front of the neat rows of boys and girls in Red House and glared unseeingly at them. The prefects in each house stood beside him, waiting for instructions on how to assist. The head boy and head girl moved from one house to the other, allocating areas.

"Red House will go to the farm" the head girl announced unceremoniously. A loud groan went round amongst the students. It was true Ojaks carried bad luck with him. Or probably because he was so mean, they always allocated difficult terrains to him, knowing he would drive the students to perform. And he recorded 100% success.

"Class one, corn farm. Class four, corn farm" he bellowed. "Class two, poultry. Class five, piggery. Class three, cassava. March" he shouted. The students turned and walked hopelessly to the next two hours of pain. Ojaks turned to the other prefects and gave brief instructions.

The walk to the farm was enough pain, and the sun was bright and hot, as though giving more reason to those who hated them. Every single student hated manual labour and Anna was sure, their school, St. Mary's Mixed School was the only private school that indulged in this abuse! But St. Mary, as their proprietress loved to be called, was of the old military stock. And the school abided by all the rules she believed in; morning duties, bedtimes, manual labours; evening preps. Huh! The only thing she did not indulge in was the morning drill. Thank goodness.

The other prefects split with the students to their various areas and allotted portions to the students. The corn farm, as it was called, was an extensive expanse of land which was not used for only corn. It was also a fruit orchid with lots of trees with shades, and to cap it all, since corn was not yet in season, there was a lot of hoeing to be done and weeding around the young stalks of corn. Each student had their own work tool. Some had rakes, some hoes and cutlasses. The class one students were sent to weed around the budding corn stalks, while class four students were sent to the open grass land.

"We can't get back before dinner today" Ata jumped up behind them as they set out to begin cutting the hard grass they had been apportioned.

"God have mercy on my poor soul" Banke chuckled.

"We know you will help us though" Anna smiled sweetly at Ata, their classmate and best male friend. Ata swung up his huge cutlass and grinned.

"That's what friends are forrrrr" he mimed, and went to work. His cutlass was sharp unlike theirs, and he swept his grass as theirs was blunt. Within minutes Ata was a few metres ahead and the girls 'waohed'.

"Better he finishes on time so he can join us" Banke said optimistically.

"Huh, aha. I'm fainting" Anna straightened slowly, sweat dripped from her hair to her face.

"Don't be weary, o woman" Banke said poetically. "Look" she said suddenly and Anna turned towards the direction of the corn rows, where Banke had indicated. Two final year boys walked towards the class. Anna recognised one of them immediately. Otto King. He was the notorious Socials Prefect. He wore his tailored blue check shirt body-fitting, and his khaki short was low-hip and baggy. The other boy had hardly been seen around Otto a lot and she didn't know his name.

"Abeg!" she hissed. She hated arrogance, and this set of prefects behaved like gods. "I hate these boys. They are so mean and arrogant. Look at how Ojaks gave class five students the piggery, that stinking place. Huh!" she exclaimed with disturbed equanimity.

"Would you have preferred he gave us?" she teased. "Hey, they are coming towards us" Banke bent quickly and continued to cut briskly. Ata chose this time to finish and straightened heartily.

"Yes," he jabbed. "Who wants to swap her supper?" he looked at Banke and Anna.

"Me, please" Anna turned to him quickly, as Otto stopped less than a metre away from them.

"You don't need to swap supper" Otto said lazily, perusing her with distressing laxity. He looked at what work she had left and smiled. Banke straightened to listen in. What did he want? Class six students were exonerated from manual labour and she couldn't wait to reach that heavenly class but this set made it even more delicious to be in.

"Hey, come here" he beckoned on Ata. "I have a job for you two" he said. "Follow me with your cutlasses" he headed towards the end of the corn farm, which was made up basically of un-cleared bush.

"Senior Ojaks is coming to inspect, senior" Anna mumbled.

"He's asked me to pick any two people I want" Otto replied looking directly into her eyes. She looked away quickly. "When Bode comes" he said, emphasizing Ojaks' real name, "tell him I called these two away. What are your names?" he asked.

"Ata"

"Anna"

"Good. Follow me"

"Wait for me" Anna whispered to Banke as they followed the two senior boys. Banke noticed a third boy also in blue house followed them.

They walked deep into the bush and Anna was only glad Ata was there. Or she would not even agree to follow them. Of course, that would have earned her a nice punishment. Finally, they stopped at a clearing with Mango trees. The Mangoes were ripening fast and the senior boys started to throw stones at them.

"I like that saying that only trees with fruits get stoned" Otto said reflexively. Ata and Anna stood listlessly, waiting for instructions. "Do you like mango, Anna?" he asked her.

"No, senior"

"Call me Otto. But only here or I'll punish you're a..., ur head off" he laughed.

"You, go over there and cut sticks" one of the other boys shouted at Ata.

"Anna, fine girl" the other boy held her wrist and pulled her closer to him.

"Leave me alone" Anna shrieked. Ata turned to look at her and stopped.

"Get out of here, idiot!" the first boy shouted at him. "Go in the bush and cut twenty sticks!!"

"Smoothen them with your big cutlass like arrows, idiot" the second boy said.

"Come and eat this mango, Anna. It really is very sweet" Otto said and bit into the ripe mango in his hand a second time. The first boy threw a stone and about four mangoes fell down.

"Make sure you note the fresh ones" Otto looked at him. "Leave Anna's hand alone, she wants to eat my mango".

"I want to eat her mango" the second boy said and they all laughed. He released her hand and she took off. Otto flew to his feet and chased her. He caught her by the waist and carried her up. She flung her blunt cutlass at him narrowly missing his face. One of the other boys twisted the cutlass out of her hand and flung it into the bush.

"Leave me alone" Anna screamed at the top of her voice. "Help me!! Nooo"

Otto dropped her under the mango tree and covered her body with his in male supremacy.

"She's so small" he laughed. He covered her mouth with a noisy kiss. "And sweet" he murmured into her mouth, effectively stifling her scream. He heard the other boys laughing as he unbuckled his belt and rolled up her dress with one hand while the other hand imprisoned her two slender wrists above her head.

"Take a rubber" one of the boys shouted.

"To hell" Otto replied just before he penetrated her. Anna's scream of pain was long and low. "Relax, girl" Otto whispered. He was slow and he took his time. And she shut him out finally.

Her eyes were shut tightly when the second person came on... and the third.

Ata sobbed in the bush, as he trashed wildly at the trees. He heard every scream for help, every sigh, snicker, laughter. He felt the pain but lacked the courage to confront the three boys. They were bigger and stronger. Above all, they were seniors. He didn't come out of the bush until he heard only the sound of silence, and peace. Peace so deceptive. She was gone.

They were all gone. And it was very dark when he finally sneaked into his dormitory.

Also an Inspired Romance:

Her Lover

Other books by the author:

Sister Minister

Strength of Character (Devotional & Workbook for Sister Minister)

52 ways to provoke God (Devotional)

The devil lied

True dream series:

Dumped

Your wish is mine

Even the lawful captive

He taketh the first

The other sister

What's good for the goose

Shattered

Scattered

Iyke's revenge

Ìka

Battered

Love come by

Novels:

Scent of water

Frail flesh

The days after that night

Tisha

Way of the unfaithful

Foreverland: A Cinderella story

Under a red delta sun

Blue dawn

Wisdom series:

Wisdom for Men

Wisdom for Pastors

Wisdom for Pastors' Wives

Wisdom for Women

Wisdom for Singles

Wisdom for Staying Married

Wisdom for Newlyweds

Issues of life series (Co-authored with Afolarin Ogúnyinka):

Somebody help! She loves my husband

Somebody help! He loves my wife

Somebody help! I'm in love

Some God Use, Some Use God

Revelation series:

Choice